MUDERLICIOUS

TRAYVON JACKSON

D1414275

PEN TALK PUBLICATIONS|SHAN PRESENTS, LLC

Copyright 2017 by

Published by Pen Talk Publications

All rights reserved

www.shanpresents.com

I would like to dedicate this unique urban novel to everyone who propels into their dreams by taking action. We could be anything we want to be if we put our minds and heart into it.
"Let's Do This!"

SYNOPSIS

Growing up in South Philadelphia, is only part of how a beautiful assassin came about. She's the best that the CIA have seen in years, and succeeds formidable missions that most barely legals her age could never think of doing. With no military experience, she does it proficiently, and doesn't leave until her targets are destroyed. She has no clue that her superiors are veterans of the CIA who're using their most lethal assassin to destroy Presidential Republican Governor Ben Scott's; run for the White House.

Having a lavish bank account doesn't always make a person content with life. She battles a mental disorder after seeing a love one's death. Seeing the investigation go cold, she makes it her duty to pursue the killer by all means; by herself. Will she find the killer or do the killer finds her? With one look in the eyes of passion a decade murder could be solved. But will she have enough time to put the dreadful puzzle together?

"An urban thriller that intensifies as the pages are turning" ----Author Trayvon D. Jackson

WISDOM

Karma is a Catch-22, like two sides of a coin. Heads or tails can't always win. Someone has to fall, lose, or welcome Karma. It's just the way life is....

Author: Trayvon D. Jackson

CHAPTER 1

The sudden downpour of heavy rain was just another sign for Tommy Gun to shut down shop in South Philly. He was the commander of the streets, and had the sister state's on lock as well. He had the top notch heroin, and crack cocaine, and was untouchable to the Feds, who desperately wanted him off of the streets. Those who knew Tommy Gun expectations knew that there was three ways — not to cross him, or else a body bag would be the only result. Fucking with his family, money, or getting over on his prostitutes would sure enough put anyone in their grave. Tommy Gun was an elegant yellow complexion, feared man who stood six-feet-three-inches, 215 pounds solid muscle.

At forty years old, with twenty years running in the game strong, without falling. He was one of the top ten richest kingpins to survive the dope game from his era. Though many knew him as an animal, and a contributor to the ridiculous murder rate. People also knew that he had a loving heart when it came to giving back to his black community. The society speculated that the commission board members protected Tommy Guns from a federal indictment. It was hard for the Feds to build a solid case on him when he had a successful rap label, pumping in millions in cash, and was neck to neck with Jay-Z's record label.

Penny House Records was known throughout the east coast releasing some of the hottest rappers from all over from Philadelphia to New York. Retiring from the dope game was being considered, but like he'd came in the game, he refused to leave it to someone who didn't deserve it. His enemies were everywhere and he even believed that they dwelled in his operation. But his power was too structured to not see trouble underneath his nose. It was twelve o'clock a.m. when Tommy Gun decided to shut down his drug operation. He moved on schedule and closed out every day at different times, so that the Feds snooping could never catch a routing pattern.

"Quavis, let's turn this bitch out, lil' homie," Tommy said to his young protégé, who was sitting at the kitchen table, feeding money into a money counting machine.

"Alright, let me wrap this back up," Quavis retorted.

"Do that while I call Ariel," Tommy Gun retorted.

Quavis was a twenty-four-year-old five-foot-eight-inch, 175-pound chocolate complexioned go-getta, and would soon be Tommy Guns replacement. Once Tommy Gun retired, he planned to move his family to Florida, and raise his two nieces from his deceased brother, who was killed years ago. Tommy Gun was grateful to have his beloved grandmother around to help him care for the kids. *Dammit, without that lady, where would I be?* Tommy Gun thought as he waited for his Pimptress to answer the phone.

"What's good, daddi?" Ariel voice boomed through the receiver of his cell phone.

"Tell me what 54th looking like?" Tommy Gun inquired of his major prostitution block, out of seven others that he owned.

"Daddi, these hoes sellin' pussy like the usual. It's green, daddi," Ariel said.

"Good, pay day tomorrow. Make sure that money come to daddi."

"I got you daddi, no worries," Ariel said, then popped a bubble gum bubble in Tommy Guns ear.

"Bitch, I hate when you do that."

"You don't be sayin' that when 'em sucking that fat ass dick of yours, and when my pussy poppin' on that dick," Ariel said sassy-like, causing Tommy Gun to chuckle. "Yeah, I kno', daddi loves that shit," Ariel retorted, smiling to herself at Tommy Gun's Keith Sweat chuckle.

"If I had to admit it, yes I do, sugar. You do kno' how to work a boy to his toes curl," Tommy Gun admitted.

"So, when can I get some?"

"Tomorrow" Tommy Gun retorted,

He and Ariel were lovers with a special bond, in spite of her being a prostitute. Pussy was like a precious stone, and if used correctly, would have you living a Boss life. From the dope game to keeping pimping alive, Tommy Gun was an intelligent mastermind.

"Tomorrow not promise—"

"Tonight not promised either, see you tomorrow baby," Tommy Gun said, then disconnected the call. Tommy Gun looked over at Quavis and saw that he was stacking the stacks of hundreds inside a duffel bag.

"Done, champ?"

"All done…$75,000 by the capsules, and $200,000 by the kilo in a day. We did good, just like all the time," Quavis explained to Tommy Gun, informing him of all the sales that occurred in one day of hustling.

"That's perfect, now let's get out of here," Tommy Gun said then headed for the front door of the apartment.

When Tommy Gun and Quavis stepped outside the apartment building, Tommy Gun walked up to his two watchers Lil' Kenny and Bo and pulled out a phat wad of cash from his Versace slacks.

"You two niggas did good tonight…" Tommy Gun said as he peeled off a thousand dollars each for Lil' Kenny and Bo, for watching his all black out Maserati GhibliQ4 and the black for jack boy's.

"Lil' Kenny, make sure you bring Brenda something special home tonight," Tommy Gun told Lil' Kenny, like he told him every other week.

"Aloma always before these streets, lil' nigga," Tommy Gun retorted as he handled the money to Lil' Kenny, the Bo.

"And Bo, make sure you do the same lil' nigga."

"I will, Tommy Gun."

"Me too, Tommy Gun," Lil' Kenny replied after Bo.

"I kno' y'all will. Now get home, and let's do this sometime tomorrow," said Tommy Gun, then walked away and towards his Maserati.

Quavis was already in his Benz truck, throwing up the peace sign to Tommy Gun. Tommy Gun in return threw up the peace sign, then turned up the volume to Drake's "Summer Sixteen" album. When he pulled off, he checked his rearview and saw Quavis pulling off in the opposite direction.

He knew Quavis would be safe going to the stash house. He had too many goons watching, and ready for a busta to attempt suicide trying to take from him. In spite of having goons at the ready, Tommy Guns wasn't naïve. He knew the consequences of slipping and underestimating anyone, could be the death of him. That's why he was always ready to take on one of his enemies, and Quavis had the same attitude. That's why he was Tommy Gun's right-hand man. And soon to be new president in South Philly.

When Tommy Gun pulled up to his grandmother Elsa's house, he saw that the kitchen light was still on, indicating that the old woman was still awake, most likely still cleaning something in the home he'd grown up in. All the money in the world couldn't get Grandmother Elsa to move into a luxurious home. Tommy Gun stepped out of the Maserati and walked up to the front door. Before he could fetch his key for the door, Grandmother Elsa opened the door with a broom in her hands

"It's 12:45 a.m. Mister, what did I tell you 'bout coming to get here this late? That girl needs all her beauty rest for school, and you're robbing her from it every time you come get here in the wee hours," Grandma Elsa whisper-shouted to Tommy Gun as he walked through the door.

"I kno' grandma, I promise it's almost over with —"

"What's that supposed to mean, Tommy?" Grandma Elsa asked

with a raised brow.

"It means I'mma have someone cover me often at the studio. So that I could have her home and in bed on time, grandma."

"That's a good one, son… remember, Elsa knows everything."

That she does! Tommy Gun thought, feeling foolish trying to throw his veteran Grandma Elsa off.

"Just stop showing up too late. I don't see why you won't just get her a nanny—"

"Grandma, we've talked about this before. I don't trust nobody around my lil' girl but you, and my mind will never change."

She knew that trying to get Tommy Gun to hire a nanny to help with Ayesha was useless. He was very overprotective of his only daughter, who he was a mother and father to. Ayesha's mother was fatally gunned down by one of Tommy Guns enemies, when Ayesha was only three years old. Though they were separated at the time, and the mother has custody of Ayesha, Tommy Gun immediately stepped in and took Ayesha, against her mother's family's protest. Despite having family on her mother's side, Ayesha wasn't fond of them. Frequent visits to her Grandmother Francis' house on the weekends ended abruptly, when Tommy Gun discovered that Francis had a child molester living under her roof. Tommy Gun loved his daughter unconditionally and spoiled her to be the Princess she was today. It was for her sake that he was preparing to retire from the game. Through all the women Tommy Gun copulated in his life, he'd only managed to spit out one gorgeous little girl that warmed his heart every time he saw her.

When he walked into the bedroom where Ayesha slept peacefully in the same bed with her two cousins, fathered by his brother. He gently tapped on her chest. Ayesha's eyes opened immediately, he loved the fact that his daughter wasn't a heavy sleeper. When she saw her father she smiled and reached out for him. Ayesha wrapped her hands around her father's neck and allowed him to scoop her out of bed, without disturbing her cousins.

"Hi daddy," Ayesha said then rested her head on her father's shoulder.

"Go back to sleep baby girl—"

"Can Alexis and Tamara come tonight, daddy?" Ayesha asked half-asleep. "Not tonight baby, tomorrow is school. How 'bout Friday?" Tommy Gun said to Ayesha.

"Okay daddy," Ayesha retorted, then closed her eyes and drifted back off to sleep, knowing that her daddy's word was trustworthy.

"See you tomorrow, grandma," Tommy Gun whispered to his grandmother as he walked out the front door and to his Maserati.

"Drive safe son," Grandma Elsa said.

"I will grandma, love you."

"Love you too, Tommy," Grandma Elsa replied.

Grandma Elsa watched Tommy Gun put Ayesha in the back seat, then hopped inside himself. As he pulled off, she waved at him as he honked his horn twice goodbye. Grandma Elsa had been around too long not to know exactly what her grandson meant by it was almost over. She just hoped that it wasn't too late, like it was for most men in the dope game. Grandma Elsa walked back inside, and said a prayer for her grandson and great granddaughter; like she did every night.

* * *

WHEN QUAVIS PULLED up to the safe house, he rubbed the sleep from his eyes. All day he'd been hustling nonstop. Then, for the most part of the night, he'd been feeding money to a counting machine, and preparing product for the next day. The job was exhausting, but he knew that he was being tested.

"Don't worry, Tommy ... I won't let you down," Quavis encouraged himself.

Quavis reached in the back seat on the passenger's floor and retrieved the duffel bag of money. He then stepped out of the Benz truck and closed the door. The rain was on and off, and he was fortunate for the light drizzle as he walked to the front door, and opened it up using his key. Inside was dark, and an empty house. No one but Quavis and Tommy Gun has access to the safe house, with a couple bodies watching it daily. They were ducked off in bushes, always ready. When Quavis walked into the safe room and flicked on the lights; he instantly saw the amiss and became alert. The room was a wreckage. The bed was upside down and the clothes in the closet were yanked from their hangers. Someone was definitely looking for the safe. Quavis dropped the duffel bag at his feet and removed his Glock 40 from his waistband. The moment he took two steps towards the closet to investigate, he froze in his tracks at the distinctive sound of the cocking back of a gun.

"What's up Quavis, looks like you've made it just in time for the party!" a familiar voice said. He was scrambling in his memory bank trying to put a face to the voice. But he and Tommy Gun had too many close enemies.

How the fuck did I get caught slipping? Quavis thought.

He was tempted to turn around and get to firing, but the uncertainty of the odds stacked against him caused him to remain calm.

Maybe they just want the money, he considered.

"Drop the gun and let's not be a hero, nigga," the familiar voice ordered Quavis.

Damn, I kno' this nigga! Quavis thought as he dropped his gun to the floor.

"You kno' what 'em here for, nigga. Open up that safe, homeboy."

With no hesitation, Quavis walked towards the closet and found the safe visible.

The wall that slid back and covered the walk-in safe was already accessed. Immediately Quavis realized that the hit was planned thoroughly. And that it was someone with bigger nits than most of their enemies.

"Hurry up nigga, before I get mad," the familiar voice said, as he pressed his gun to the back of Quavis' head.

Quavis sighed, then began to access the safes code hitting numbers 24-18-20-19. When the safe opened up, Quavis spun around quickly, attempting to take the gunman off-guard, but was stopped short as the gunman squeezed the trigger, catching Quavis in his face and forehead.

"I told you no hero shit, nigga," the gunman said then pumped two more slugs into Quavis' skull.

Boom! Boom!

* * *

AYESHA DIDN'T KNOW what awoke her in the wee hours, her bladder or the amiss in the air that she couldn't describe. She emerged from bed and walked out into the hallway on her way to the bathroom until she heard her father's voice raise.

"Motherfucka, you want live to see tomorrow young ass nigga?" Ayesha heard her father shout. Ayesha walked pass the bathroom and downstairs. She hated when her daddy was upset. He was good at hiding it when in her presence, but she knew him well. Especially when she knew her father like no one, other than her Grandma Elsa.

When Ayesha came downstairs and walked into the spacious kitchen, she wasn't prepared to see what she saw. Her father was bound to a chair with a bloody, battered face, surrounded by two gunmen in all black attire, wearing ski masks over their faces. It was useless for them, because Tommy Gun knew who the two masked men were. Seeing her daddy smile with a bloody grill momentarily calmed her, until of the gunmen slapped him with his pistol.

"Daddy!" Ayesha screamed as she ran towards her daddy.

"Ayesha no!" Tommy Gun shouted, seeing the love of his life being lifted off of her by the second gunman.

"Don't hurt her Youngin'. I'll give you everything, just spare my daughter, man," Tommy Gun begged.

Damn, he's good, the second gunmen thought.

"Well let's do this, then," The goon known as Youngin' said, who was the Mastermind behind taking Tommy Gun out, which would profit him big in the future. He held Ayesha from behind, who couldn't stop the cascading tears if she tried to. She was afraid for her father, never once thinking about her own safety. Ayesha was too young to understand that her life was changing forever. *I can't let him hurt my baby girl,* Tommy Gun thought.

"Please Youngin' let her go," Tommy Gun begged

8

Does he know it's me? ... hell naw'll, thought Youngin'.

"Talk nigga, you know how this goes. Who is the connect, nigga?" Youngin' asked as he walked closer to Tommy Gun, and let Ayesha go. Ayesha ran up to her daddy and hopped into his lap, where she hugged him like it was the last hug she would ever give him. With his blood smeared on her face, she could smell the coverage her daddy had even in a perilous situation.

"Daddy, get them out of here!" Ayesha cried.

"Just chill, baby girl ... let daddy handle business," Tommy Gun said to Ayesha, then looked up at his two enemies. He noticed how the second gunman didn't say nothing since his arrival.

It didn't take Tommy Gun long to discover the infiltration. He knew exactly who was behind the mask, inspite of their incognito approach. Tommy Gun paid attention to everyone that he came in contact with. The nefarious cat he knew as Youngin' wasn't fooling anyone. Nor did the chubby gunman perplex him. What surprised him was that he would have never expected Youngin' to invade his home impudently. Tommy Gun had signed Youngin' to his label, and had him living lavish at just eighteen years old.

And now, he was crossing Tommy Gun.

"Youngin'..." Tommy Gun called out his attackers' name. "My connect's name is Juan, the same Juan from Benz Carlot —"

Boom! Boom! Boom!... It was all Youngin' needed to hear come out of Tommy Guns mouth. He pulled the trigger, sending Tommy Guns blood and brain juice in a splatter onto eight-year-old Ayesha. She was shocked as she stared at her daddy's lifeless, bloody face. When Ayesha turned around and looked Youngin' in his cold eyes. She wanted to make him pay for taking her daddy away from her. But when she went to move she couldn't, her legs were not operating with her mind.

"Let's go, Fat Boy," Youngin' said, the turned on his heels and left Tommy Guns mansion in East Philly, with his new right-hand man. Ayesha cried for hours as her daddy stiffened from rigor mortis setting in. It was dawn before she was able to leave her daddy side and called the closest relative, and only relative she trusted, Grandma Elsa.

CHAPTER 2

The going away for Tommy Vantrell Jordan was a tremendous one. The St. John Church of God on 12th and Pinewood was stretching out five blocks from the church. It was no secret to everyone that a legend was leaving the streets. Since the news hit of Tommy Gun's death and Quavis', the murder rate went sky high. Every night, there were a couple murders on just one block. His loyal men were out hunting for any clue to whom was responsible for his death. But they were no better than the happy detectives, who were so anxious to close the case quickly as a cold case file. The streets, if they did know something, were living by the code: see no evil, speak no evil, hear no evil.

The funeral was very emotional, and everyone gave their warm condolences to Grandma Elsa and Ayesha, who sat in the first row as the church reviewed Tommy Guns body. As the church choir sang "I'll Fly Away," Ayesha cried in her grandmother's arms. Sitting next to Ayesha, to her left, were her two cousins Alexis and Tamara, who were all the family she had left, besides Grandma Elsa. They, too, were crying and grieving the loss of the uncle, who'd taken care of them since their father was killed. Neither girls were too young to realize that the backbone to their family was gone.

There wouldn't be any more grab what you wanted at the mall, nor picking out the newest model of clothes and shoes. Not with Grandma Elsa, who was strictly against purchasing material items with drug money. She was too much of a vet to except that Tommy Guns money came mainly from his record label. Grandma Elsa wanted nothing to do with Tommy Guns establishment. So she laid off his employment and sold the building to the bank. Grandma Elsa took the 5.5 million dollars from the record label and placed it on CD's in the bank for Ayesha, who couldn't touch the money until she turned eighteen. Until then, the money that Grandma Elsa did have would get the girls through school and afford them a comfortable education, and nothing more. Ayesha and her cousins had no clue that hence forward, everything that they got would be because they worked hard for it, to earn it,

Grandma Elsa, like others, was worried about Ayesha being effected by Tommy Guns death. So she hired a psychotherapist to examine her, just in case she was suffering from nightmares. Despite hiring a psychotherapist, Grandma Elsa was moved to see how strong Ayesha was. Though Ayesha was more quiet than usual, it was the only transformation that she'd espied of her granddaughter.

When Ayesha saw the funeral assistants walking towards her and Grandma Elsa, she knew that it was their time to say their final goodbyes to her father.

"It's time to say goodbye baby," Grandma Elsa whispered to Ayesha.

"Yes ma'am," Ayesha replied while wiping her eyes. She then looked over at Alexis and Tamara, who were crying, and knew as well that the time to say goodbye to Uncle Tommy had come. When the lid shut closed on the grey casket, Ayesha knew, like everyone in the church, that it would be the last time she saw Tommy Vantrell Jordan in the flesh. The funeral assistants helped Grandma Elsa to her feet, and she helped Ayesha to hers.

"Come on Alexis and Tamara, say goodbye to your uncle," Grandma Elsa said to her granddaughters.

Alexis and Tamara both stood and came to Grandma Elsa's side.

Together, they all walked up to the open half-mast casket. Ayesha stared at her father and took in every detail of him. The make up hid the battered face she'd last seen of him, and the bullet hole to his forehead that killed him was only visible to the naked eye. If not for the news informing the entire city that his brains were shot out the back of his head, no one would've noticed the repair work on his forehead. Ayesha could still feel the warm blood that splattered on her face when her daddy was shot. She held onto him, crying for hours, wanting to go after her daddy killers, but her eyes wouldn't allow her to leave her daddy alone,

Ayesha wanted the killer to pay badly, but she couldn't find the man with the mask on, with the creepy evil looking eyes. The impact of losing Tommy Gun wouldn't hit her until she was old enough to understand it. Ayesha rubbed her daddy's hard, cold hands, and noticed that his costly Rolex was gone from his wrist.

"Grandma, where is daddy's watch?" Ayesha shouted over the choir singing. Grandma Elsa bent down to Ayesha's level and whispered in her ear.

"God has too much gold in heaven, baby. There's no need for him to bring nothing from this world, but his soul. Your daddy is looking down smiling at us now, and that's a wonderful jewel."

Grandma Elsa was too straightforward when it came to her raising anyone in her household. At seventy-five years old, she did it as a single parent raising Tommy and Willie without their father, who was killed by the police, and was Grandma Elsa's only child. Tommy and Willie had learned a lot from Grandma Elsa's prudence. They just chose to bear fruit from the forbidden tree in life, and lost their lives behind their decision. They both had college degrees and could have been anything in the world besides thugs in the streets. Grandma Elsa didn't know how she was going to raise three eight-year-old girls alone. But she would do her best to make sure they were well taken care of, and educated to take the right path in life. Ayesha looked over at Alexis and Tamara and saw them still crying, as they looked at their favorite uncle for the last time. She then looked up at Grandma Elsa, who was looking down at her smiling.

"Can I kiss him, Grandma?" Ayesha asked

"Go ahead baby … kiss your father goodbye!" Grandma Elsa retorted. As Ayesha stood on her tiptoes, a funeral assistant lifted her off of her feet, and allowed her to kiss her father on his forehead. When she was done, Ayesha came over to her father ear and whispered to him.

"I love you daddy … I'mma make the man with the mask pay."

It was a promise she vowed to fulfill by all means.

CHAPTER 3

TEN YEARS LATER:

"*B*aby, you gotta teach them hoes how to not play with that money. When yo' momma was out there they respected my Pimptress —"

"Ma, that's ten years ago, and these streets have changed dramatically since then.," Bianca said to her mother Ariel, who was now a retired vet to the prostitution, and was trying to show twenty-eight-year-old, beautiful Bianca the ropes of the game when money was being played with.

"Woman, ten years ago don't do nothing but change the economy, not the attitude and class of a boss bitch," Ariel said to Bianca, then blew cigarette smoke in her face.

"Mom ... really?" Bianca said, fanning the smoke out of her face as she stood at the dresser in her room, checking her makeover out in the mirror, before she stepped out into the night to control her prostitute's.

"Child, smoke only makes you stay younger. When you stop is when it kills you," Ariel said to Bianca, who was now checking out her fat ass protruding from her $7,000 leather tight fitting pants. At five-feet-five inches, 125 pounds with a flawless red skin complexion, Bianca knew undisputed that she was a badass bitch.

Smack!

"Yeah baby girl, you have all that moma gave ya," Ariel said after slapping Bianca on her ass.

"Thanks ma ..." Bianca said the kissed her mom on both of her cheeks.

"I'mma check these hoes tonight, and strip they ass before I let them go!" Bianca informed her mother that she would heed her advice.

The prostitution operation was all they had that was bringing in cash and paying the rent at their luxurious condo in South Philly. Since the age of eighteen, Bianca had been using the power of her body to get what she wanted in the world. Ariel wasted no time schooling Bianca of the essence of her body. She was now twenty-eight, and a professional Pimptress, known throughout Philadelphia, who only dealt with six figured men who were down to pay for the worthwhile. Not knowing her white father, who'd been Ariel's client at the time, she was only living for her mother and her. Who was her world and taught her everything she knew about being a diva Pimptress.

"Well I'll see you in the morning, and breakfast is on you, Ma," Bianca said as she grabbed her purse and keys, then strutted out of her room to the front door.

"I guess child—"

"No mom, don't do that, because you know when I could I be in that kitchen making sure yo' feet don't even hit the ground before you've eaten breakfast," Bianca reminded her mother of her generosity.

"Okay baby, breakfast on me. Now go get that money," Ariel waved Bianca off as she sat down on the plush leather sofa.

There was no need for Bianca to check for assistance. She trusted her mother word more than gold. Something that Ariel had taught her strongly to me by no matter what. When Bianca was gone out into the night, Ariel twisted her a Kush blunt, and prepared to watch the B.E.T. Awards. Ariel, at only forty-six years old, had her run in the prostitution business until she had nothing more than good oral sex to offer her clients. The drugs had aged her beauty, and her health was constantly failing her. She was fortunate to escape any STD's and she only had Tommy Gun to think for it who made sure she was always careful.

"Damn, I miss that man," Ariel said amongst herself, with Tommy Gun on her mind.

She could remember the night ten years ago when she'd last talked to him. *It's sad, but it's life,* Ariel thought. Ariel, like everyone else, knew that the killer wanted Tommy Gun out the way. A lot of hustlers wanted him out the way, which only made it hard for anybody to single out the killer. Everybody suspected someone close to him, other than Quavis. But Ariel knew those speculations were without merit, because the only person that was like give to him was his beautiful daughter and family. Ariel, herself, was a suspect but was never questioned about his death by anyone. She continued to do her thing on 54th to 61st, banking serious cash in prostitution. She kept her ears open and eyes on the up and coming ballers. But she never smelled any signs of Tommy Gun and Quavis' killer. *That night, the goons that were watching their backs were even killed, which meant that someone came with their A-game while Tommy Gun's guard was down,* Ariel thought as she exhaled smoke from her nostrils. Ariel planned the innocent role in Tommy Gun's death thoroughly. And would take the truth to her grave....

"Now that's my boy," She said when she saw Philadelphia's hottest rapper's new music pop up. His name was Young Zoe.

"Tommy Gun would be proud of you boy, if he was here to see your success," Ariel said as she turned up the volume to the flat screen TV, and watched Young Zoe represent South Philly.

Ten years ago, he was with Tommy Gun's record label until his death, when he the ventured on his own as a solo artist and feared man. Ariel loved him because he kept the traits of what Tommy Gun had taught him. He took care of his people just like Tommy Gun did.

Now he was stacking six figures next to Jay-Z and Beyoncé. Ariel loved those who came from the struggle and never gave up. Tommy Gun's death was a setback to a lot of potential stars, but they gave up instead of going at it with everything that the Master taught them up until his death.

I always told him that he would be more than he set out to be if he just kept pushing them mixtapes, now look where you at nigga. You putting Phil-adelphia in its own class, Ariel thought as she bobbed her head to Young Zoe's music while sanging his lyrics.

"(Insert Music Symbol) The heart of Philly nigga – South Philly taking the streets from bears/walking on their bare skin/Philly nigga just getting it in/ (Insert Music Symbol)"

* * *

WAITING three months after her eighteenth birthday just to touch wealth her father put up for her was the most anxious time of her life. Ayesha not felt like a grown woman and the dive of South Philly. She wasn't a little innocent girl and the diva of South Philly. She wasn't a little innocent girl anymore, and had every means of keeping up her reputation. She stood five-feet-nine-inches with hips, thighs, and an ass to run a man insane. Her flawless yellow skin was her meal ticket to the ballers' and small-time hustlers' stash alone with her striking beauty. But let not the looks fool you. If someone got Ayesha time wrong, she was a black belt mix martial arts champion, who'd embarrassed enough men who'd tried to treat her like some ordinary chick, who was hooked on the click and money. She loved those types, especially when she knocked them out, then took all of their bank roll.

Despite not going to college after high school like Alexis and Tamara did, who were in law school working to be lawyers, Ayesha was a brilliant woman in all aspects. Grandma Elsa still felt that she should go to college, but Ayesha was a woman who'd made her mind up, her freshman year in high school, that college was not in her plans. What Grandma didn't know was that her granddaughter was a woman way before she became a freshman, getting away with a lot of dirt underneath Grandma Elsa's nose.

At fourteen, Ayesha was sneaking out with men double her age, and having sex with them for extra money to be in her pockets. Being rich at eighteen was torture to her mind, when she wanted it now. The kids her age tried with their all to make her their girlfriend, but was nowhere near her expectations. She was doing everything but being an open prostitute. She picked her man fitting her expectations, and stuck with him until his well went dry, or he was arrested and had to go do time. She wasn't the ride or die chick that she portrayed, and it costed her many confrontations when one of her exes was released and saw her on the next hustler arm. Grandma Elsa had no clue of what her old-fashioned raising had done to innocent little Ayesha. She was addicted to sex, and money, and went by the code name "Murderlicious." She was the best that anyone could hire for murder.

Seeing her father killed ten years ago was the birth of a vicious woman that stayed on the go, eager for her next hill. To know Murderlicious, a person had to know money and the Master who'd taught her how to move like a ghost. Ayesha stepped out of the hot steaming, soothing shower and grabbed her towel off its rack. As she dried off, she looked at herself in the mirror and admired her sexy body like she did every night. Her lean slim waisted 145-pound frame was a gift from God.

"I kno' 'em a bad bitch... but you can't have me, Master," Ayesha said reiterating what she'd said to her last kill hours ago in New York. He was an old, fat black man who worked as a lobbyist, who the Master superiors needed assassinated. He was an easy kill, like it was told he would be. With a seductive blink of her eyes, and a sexy pout, she had him ready to fuck her in the ballroom. But she'd lured him to the women's restroom, just outside where they exchanged numbers, and agreed to meet at his hotel suite. At the hotel, business came before pleasure. Ayesha sucked his dick until he was spitting out cross sea's accounts. She slit the man's throat and cut his dick off in 1.2 seconds, then stuffed his mutilated dick down his throat.

"That motherfucka thought he had a come up, huh?" Ayesha said to herself, the walked into her plush bathroom.

When she looked at the time, she saw that 2:45a.m. was illuminating from her clock in red digits on her nightstand. She needed to rest for tomorrow, before she booked a flight to Dallas, Texas, to carry out another kill. Ayesha slid on comfortable lingerie, then climbed in bed. Before she closed her eyes, Ayesha grabbed the small picture frame holding her father's picture of him holding her in his arms when she was seven. It was her favorite picture of him and was her lucky charm.

For years she'd been looking for answers to her father's death that could lead her to his killer. She could still remember her daddy blood splattering on her face. She'd heard the rumors of her father's operations from some of the older men she slept with. She never revealed to any of her exes that Tommy Gun was her father. She was ashamed to tell them, because she wasn't an epitome of a boss nigga's daughter. All that he'd worked hard for was sold to the bank on the first auction bid. And what she had, as far as real money, was stuck in CD's until she'd turned eighteen. The rumors she'd heard surrounding her father's death weren't substantial enough to pick out anyone as the killer. *Everyone suspected that it was someone close to him, but who's to say all his enemies weren't close?* Ayesha thought.

"Don't worry daddy, one day I will have him ... I promise, someone will slip up and give me everything," Ayesha said, then placed the picture frame back on the nightstand. She then reached underneath her pillow and smiled when she felt her two Glock H5's.

"My babies," Ayesha said, then closed her eyes.

She clapped her hands twice and all lights in her condo that were on instantly died, and her house alarm was automatically set, assessing her four-digit pass code all at once. Ayesha was high class in a lot of aspects, and it all came from having to struggle for the life she deserved, but was robbed of. She was completely different from Alexis and Tamara, who were complacent with the struggle, and would rather go without if they didn't have it. But many times, Ayesha wouldn't let them miss out on the joy of having money their pockets.

They knew what Ayesha was doing when she would sneak out in the middle of the night on a school night with one of her boyfriends. Alexis and Tamara were surprised that Ayesha didn't end up pregnant like most girls her age who were doing worse than her.

Ayesha was different from the young women who'd gotten knotted up by their thug life boyfriends. Most of the pregnant girls at a young age in South Philadelphia loved their boyfriends and purposely got pregnant thinking that they would always be together. Ayesha didn't love any man, but her father. She was cold-hearted and definitely out for only their money and a good fuck. Anything further was going against her standards and expectations. That's why she wasn't a teen mom and out in the world alone, left to raise a snotty nose by herself. She had no empathy, not even for a compassionate man. And the only man she trusted today was her Master, who'd taught her everything she needed to know since she was nine years old, and who'd chosen her code name for hire to murder – "Murderlicious."

* * *

WHEN MIKE P. finished fucking the prostitute named Rosa, he cleaned himself up and paid her a $1,000 for the good head and pussy she gave him. She was his favorite and was always on time for him. After fucking five different me, she still had enough fire to exhaust Mike P., who was a small-time hustler in South Philly.

"Thank you, daddy," Rosa said as she counted the crumbled wad of cash that summed precisely $1,000.

"Naw'll thank you, baby girl. Sometime tomorrow," Mike P. said as he tucked his .357 pistol in the back waistband of his jeans.

"Same time, daddy," Rosa retorted, then strutted off to the bathroom to clean up and prepare for her next client. As she walked to the bathroom, Mike P. stared at her caramel curvaceous body, and wanted to take another round with the Puerto Rican prostitute. But he had money to replace. The cash he'd just broke Rosa off with.

Damn that bitch kno' she's bad as hell, Mike P. said then exited the hotel suite.

When Mike P. stepped on the elevator and as the doors were closing, two men stopped the door and aimed their glocks at him. They both wore ski masks on their faces. Mike P. found himself in trouble.

"What's up, son?" one of the men spoke.

Mike P. was speechless and the only dumb thing that he could think of in attempt to evade the threat was reach for his .357. The move cost him his life, after the first bullet went through his forehead and splattered his brains on the back walls of the elevator.

"Young Zoe say he even now, son," one of the men said, who shot Mike P. He pumped two more slugs in Mike P., then fled with his partner.

Rosa, like everyone on the third floor of the hotel, heard the shots. But it was South Philly, where shots were heard every night. Everyone was accustomed to the fusillades and all-night crime scenes. The people in the community's understanding was all on cue: See no evil, speak no evil, hear no evil.

Mike P. was a small-time hustler who'd tried elevating his game by fronting a kilo of heroin from Young Zoe's organization. After months of avoiding to pay up for the front, Young Zoe sent his goons to wash Mike P. up. Young Zoe was a powerful man who showed the hood mad love. But like he was taught by his mentor Tommy Gun, a man only had one chance to cross him, and cheating him out of any money, no matter what the amount was, was cheating him and cheating him was crossing him. Consequently, Mike P., at only eighteen years old had no option other than paying with his life for the cardinal mistake.

CHAPTER 4

*A*yesha stepped off the Greyhound bus at the Philadelphia bus station in downtown South Philly and spotted her Masters Lincoln Town Car parked in the meter zone. With her small luggage in hand, Ayesha walked over to the meter, paid the parking fee, then hopped inside the passenger seat, placing her luggage between her legs. The Master then pulled off into traffic.

"So how was it in Dallas, young lady?" Ayesha's Master asked.

He was an old, black man, extremely dark with a head full of grey hair, and a Master of Japanese Martial Arts. Other than Master, he was known as Mr. Bernard King. Some folks called him Smoke from the old days. At sixty-five years old, the old man had a lot of respect from powerful people across the world, like the CIA Special Opps Unit, and had connections to the underground world, where his association with crooked CIA officials existed. For ten years, he'd been Ayesha's psychotherapist, and had helped her deal with the death of her father.

"It was a good one, sir...one shot, one kill, and it was over with," Ayesha informed her Master of her latest kill in Dallas, Texas of a white man running for the D.A.'s office, and someone who the CIA wanted dead, and not in the District Attorney's office.

"It'll be a couple of days before they find him, sir," Ayesha informed her Master.

"That's perfect... you did a good job. In a couple days, you'll be receiving a call; listen to all the instructions and proceed with an execution.

"Okay, sir," Ayesha retorted,

"Tonight, I want you to report to the gym at 9:00 p.m., you'll be sparring with another black belt from Atlanta, Georgia. They say she's a tough one."

"Well, we'll just see how tough she is tonight, sir," Ayesha said then smiled at the Master.

The Master had no doubt that Ayesha would destroy the girl. He hadn't seen Ayesha's kind in a while. And with ten years of training her, it was as if he'd spit her out himself. He wanted her to go pro and earn a world champion belt.

But Ayesha wasn't fond to gaining publicity. She wanted kills, and not fans raving her name. The Master dropped Ayesha off at her plush condo, and handed her the money she'd earned for the last kill. The kill put her bank to an additional $50,000.

When Ayesha stepped inside her condo, she tossed her luggage onto her plush leather sofa, and unlaced her Adidas sneakers. She felt good to be back home again. When she slid her shoes off, and walked on the plush carpet to the kitchen. She realized that she was due for some male company. In the kitchen, she hit the red flashing button to her answering machine, and listened to her messages from those who didn't have her cellular number.

"What's up, Ayesha? this Tony, call me when you get a chance" – *BEEP!*

"What's good, baby? this Brandon. I been thinking about you, hit me up when you get a chance –"

Now Brandon knows exactly how to fuck a bitch's brains out," Ayesha said as she poured herself a glass of orange juice from the refrigerator.

BEEP!

"Hey, this is Mr. Melvin, call me when you can. I have them tools you needed."

BEEP!

"End of messages," the automated voice announced.

"Good," Ayesha said, excited to her Melvin's voice. He was her gun connect and had finally got her orders of silencers in, something she always wanted to have in store. Ayesha picked up the cordless phone and returned Mr. Melvin's call. The phone rang twice before he answered.

"Hello, who's calling?"

"Someone you're expecting, how's everything?" Ayesha asked.

Mr. Melvin knew the distinctive sexy voice from anybody. And she was right, he was expecting her to call him. He just wished they could talk more business opportunities than firearms. He wanted to fuck her like no man has never done, and make her cry out his name as she came to her orgasm. But he was a married man, and she wasn't interested in 300-pound men.

"Yes lady, I've been expecting you ... I have everything you've requested. I had to grab them from a Russian —"

"That's good, Sir. I don't need to know of your service ... when can you deliver them to me?" Ayesha asked,

"Deliver?" Why can't you just stop by and pick them up?" Mr. Melvin asked. He wanted to see Ayesha. It made his day, and Ayesha knew it herself. With a smile on her face she said, "Because I'mma be too busy with my date, Sir. I will transfer the money ahead of time today. You just make sure they get to me, Sir, okay." Ayesha, still smiling, could see Mr. Melvin sad face slouching.

"Okay Ms. Jordan, I will have them delivered as soon as possible," Mr. Melvin said.

"Thank you, Sir," Ayesha replied, then hung up the phone. She then called Brandon's phone and got him on the third ring.

"What's up, baby?" Brandon spoke, already knowing it was Ayesha from his caller ID.

"What's up with you? Will you be able to stop by?" Ayesha said seductively.

"What time, baby?"

"Now," Ayesha demanded, then hung up the phone. She'd met Brandon a few months ago at a Beyoncé concert in East Philly. She loved concerts and attended all of them that came to Philadelphia. Ayesha walked upstairs and hopped into a soothing, hot shower, bathing herself with strawberry fragrance body wash, so that she could smell good for Brandon and taste delicious to him when he savored her body and juicy mound.

* * *

"Yo son, we gonna run, them adlibs after lunch break," Young Zoe said to his engineer named, Derick through his mic.

"We cool with that, boss man," Derick retorted.

Young Zoe placed the headphones made by Doctor Dre on the mic then walked out of the recording booth. When Young Zoe stepped into the hall, three men from his entourage rushed him offering a bottle of water, a phat blunt of purple haze, and a towel to throw over his head. Everywhere Young Zoe went, he kept an entourage of huge men that were six-foot-five and 250 pounds solid. He was the star of Philly, all over, and was well protected by the best bodyguards out of South Philly.

"Boss is waiting on you to call him. I told him you would call him back once you go done recording," Young Zoe's head man of his entourage named Bone informed him as they walked out the back door to the recording studio.

"Thanks Bone, I'll give him a call right away," Young Zoe retorted. Boss was Young Zoe's main man controlling his drug organization and who had been around since Young Zoe muscled the streets from his mentor – Tommy Gun.

Young Zoe hopped into the back seat of his all black and armored Hummer H2 and immediately called up Boss.

"Downtown Ceci's Pizza," Young Zoe directed his driver Mac, while waiting for Boss to answer.

"Yes sir, boss man," Mac retorted the pulled off with a backup

Hummer behind them. Young Zoe moved with precautions everywhere he went. He was a powerful man, but even the powerful men have enemies who are anticipating a slip up. The night he took Tommy Gun out was an easy task, because of Tommy Gun's lack of heavy security around him. Young Zoe and Boss only had to kill two men at the safe house, then waited on Quavis to show up. Then, another two men at the mansion where he killed Tommy Gun in front of his daughter. Boss didn't answer the phone, so Young Zoe decided to leave him a message.

"I'm open tonight, hit me back with what's good, nigga," Young Zoe said, then hung the phone up.

As he puffed on the blunt, Young Zoe's mind went back to thinking of his demand of South Philly. He couldn't believe that it'd already been ten years since that night. He'd planned it carefully with Boss, who he'd met in the DC area, when visiting family members in Washington, DC. Ten years ago, Boss' name was Fat Boy. Everyone knew he was trying to make a name in the rap game. Young Zoe was honest with Fat Boy whose music became a flop. He saw better potential in Fat Boy, and it wasn't music. He needed him as a shield and someone who would bring a new era to Philly. People feared Boss, much as they feared Young Zoe, who everyone knew was behind Boss 100%.

As the Hummer H2 pulled into Ceci's Pizza Restaurant, Young Zoe prepared himself for the cameras and fans who would be in the area. He loved the celebrity fame, and had worked hard for it. He wasn't the skimpy eighteen-year-old, goon and rapper that he was ten years ago. He was now five-foot-eight-inches, 175 pounds solid, with a peanut butter complexion, and his own damn boss. There was no special lady in his life. Shit, to him, all the women were accessible to him. Every night, he had a different woman in his bed, and quickly dismissed them at sunrise.

"Do you want us to keep it running, boss?" Mac asked.

"Naw'll, just relax. I'mma be in for a lil' longer than usual ... I gotta handle some business," Young Zoe informed Mac, while rubbing his shadow beard.

"Okay, boss man, Mac retorted.

When Young Zoe stepped out of the Hummer H2, his entourage was already there awaiting him. The camera's flashed and fans screamed out his name.

"Young Zoe, I love you!"

"Can we have yo' photograph?!"

It took Young Zoe a half hour before he made it inside the restaurant and sat down at his booth. While he was eating, he got a call from Boss informing him that Mike P. was handled like he'd ordered.

* * *

SARAH KRAKOWSKI THOUGHT that she would destroy the underground black belt when she first saw her. But the moment she began sparring off with Ayesha, and couldn't get inside her defense, those thoughts of victory quickly vanished. For thirty minutes now, she'd been shut down by Ayesha, and she was the champion of the world. Sarah realized that she was fortunate to not be on national TV defending her title against Ayesha, because she was nowhere on the winning side. Ayesha saw the kick before it was even executed, and weaved the Russian, simultaneously delivering a high kick to Sarah's head, causing her to stumble backwards. Sarah was grateful for the helmet, or else it would have been lights out for her, because that kick was meant for her temple.

"Watch them legs woman, they're like lighting!" Sarah's manager and trainer yelled at her.

"Smoke, you didn't tell me that you had a monster. You just said she was good, pal," Sarah's manager said to the Master, who he'd known for years.

"I almost told you, Patrick, that she was the best," said the Master as they watched Ayesha continue to defeat Sarah.

"Why won't she go for the money, Smoke?" Patrick asked with dollar signs in his eyes.

"It's not what she wants to do. To her it's just the sport and a medication tool, pal."

"Block that kick, Sarah!" Patrick yelled to Sarah who missed the could be fatal kick to her left temple. Once again, she was thanking the helmet for support.

"$200 million I'll give her up front. That's more than what I started Sarah off with, before I knew she was a champ," Patrick offered. The Master looked at the old white man who was a black belt himself in martial arts.

"Patrick, when I say this woman don't see the money, I mean she don't see the money. This is just a meditation for her, which makes me the best psychotherapist in the world ... I guess, huh?" said the Master.

When both managers looked up at the dead silence of feet shuffling. They saw Ayesha with her foot pinning Sarah's face to the deck.

"Shit man," Patrick said, then clapped his hands, ashamed for Sarah himself.

"Done ladies, you two did very well," said Patrick as he walked onto the padded floor to help Sarah to her feet. The Master followed with a towel and bottle of water that he tossed to Ayesha.

"Thanks, Mr. King," Ayesha said, then took a swig of cold water. When she screwed the top back on, she wiped the sweat from her face.

"You're good, why don't you go for the tittle?" Sarah asked after she removed her helmet.

"It's not the sport that I do it for, it's how I think," Ayesha said breathing heavily, trying to catch her wind.

"You defeated the champion of the world, young lady. You have a gift when you're ready—"

"No, thank you. Like I said, it's not what I want to get into," Ayesha said to Patrick who became speechless.

"Well, we're done here. We'll meet again, Smoke," Patrick said, then offered his hand to shake Ayesha's.

"Whatever keeps you moving, continue to do it. In my eyes, you are a champion, woman," Patrick said as he shook Ayesha's hand.

"Thank you, sir," Ayesha responded, then shook Sarah's hand.

"I'll be watching you Sunday. I'm confident to say that you will kick her ass," Ayesha said.

"Thank you, I will do just that," Sarah retorted.

When Patrick and Sarah drove away in their limousine, Ayesha and the Master sparred off for another thirty minutes. Like always, the Master barely got his win in against the monster he'd created. Ayesha showered at the gym, then retired at her condo where she rested well until dawn came around.

CHAPTER 5

$\mathcal{T}$he call she'd been anticipating couldn't come any sooner than breakfast. Ayesha talked with her hire for murder representative and confirmed her code name, then listened to the instructions to carry out her hit. After receiving all the information she needed, Ayesha looked up her target on her data, and quickly studied his background. She was surprised to see how important he was to the Presidential run for the White House. She had no clue why he was wanted dead, and she cared less who wanted him dead. Her only concern was to carry out the hit and get back to Philadelphia.

Ayesha stepped off the plane at JFL Airport with her small luggage inside a black duffel bag, and strutted to the waiting lobby. After getting cleared to leave the airport, Ayesha hauted a cab and handed him $50 dollars.

"First Hilton sir, keep the change," Ayesha said to the Arab driver.

"Thank you so much, lady," the Arab driver said, grateful for the extra change in the busy city. As the cab drove through the rush hour traffic, Ayesha took in the beautiful sight of New York City. It wasn't like Philadelphia where folks were afraid to visit, and only loved to come see the Philadelphia Eagles play football. *Alexis and Tamara were in New York. Maybe I'll stop by and check on them before I leave,* Ayesha thought, realizing how much she'd missed her cousins. Being on the run all the time, she rarely had time to check in with her family – not even Grandma Elsa.

"We're at the Hilton, young lady," the Arab informed Ayesha, who was spaced out in her thoughts.

"Thank you, sir," Ayesha said, then exited the cab with her duffel bag.

Ayesha walked inside the Hilton hotel and checked into a room. Once inside, she removed her Verizon Track Phone from her duffel bag and called her representative. On the first ring, an automated voice answered the phone.

"Please enter your code name." –*Beep!*

Ayesha punched in her code name – Murderlicious.

"Thank you, now please wait for your representative," the automated voice said to Ayesha, then put her on hold with Jazz music in the background.

Two minutes had passed before a familiar voice come on the line.

"I reckon you've made it safely."

"Yes, I have. I'm at the Hilton on Jefferson," Ayesha gave her location to her representative.

"Okay, what room?" he asked

"Room #212."

"Ten minutes, someone will drop off your tools. Get the job done and be careful," her representative informed her, then hung up the phone. Ayesha grabbed her bag and dumped all her clothes on the bed. She sorted her shower necessities out and waited for her guest. When the knocks came at the door, Ayesha walked over and opened it up. She saw a white man in a suit with shades on his face holding a briefcase.

"Murderlicious?" he asked for assurance.

"Yes."

"Here … good luck," the man in the suit said as he handed over the briefcase to Ayesha, then walked away.

Ayesha closed the door and came back inside the room. She placed the briefcase on the bed and opened it up.

"Damn," Ayesha exclaimed as she stared at the beautiful M21 sniper rifle.

"Now this bitch is a beautiful bitch," Ayesha said, then put the rifle together for a test run.

* * *

MADISON SQUARE GARDENS had a crowd exhilarating like no other sold out concert for Young Zoe when he took the stage.

"I see y'all Madison Square!" Young Zoe screamed into the mic while pointing at the immense audience. The women were shouting out his name, lusting off his eight pack and million-dollar platinum chain that sparkled scintillating diamonds that read: Young Zoe.

"We gone get this money. Yo' DJ, will, drop that beat," Young Zoe ordered the DJ who immediately dropped the number one hit, that made him the man he was today.

"(Insert music note) Us Philly niggas get money ... oh my gosh! We get money, click, clack we get money, ski masks we get money! (insert music note)" Young Zoe crunked the crowd, performing his hit. Scanning the faces of his fans as they serenaded with him.

"This Philly nigga got what? (music note)" Young Zoe asked the crowd.

"Money, hoe's, and problems for you foe's!" the crowd shout back.

Boss and the rest of his Philadelphia entourage stood front row, supporting Young Zoe with his fans. They were his number one fans, and the face of Philly. Boss loved seeing Young Zoe perform, though sometimes it got to him that he couldn't take the stage with him. *In times like this, I just wish I would have gave it my all instead of giving up so easy,* Boss thought as he watched his boy perform his next hit called, "Soldier Girl." It was a hit for the ladies who had a hustler as a man, and had the entire city of Philly addicted. Everywhere Boss and his entourage went, he heard the song playing. *My nigga the truth!* Boss thought then got in with the exhilarating crowd that sung along.

"(insert music note) Say a soldier who keep Nina on her hip/a real soldier who cook meals yearly/a soldier who moan and bit like she eating a T-Bone steak (music note)," Young Zoe rapped to his immense crowd of fans.

* * *

CONSTITUTIONAL PHILANTHROPIST LAWYER ERIC BOWER moved through his law firm gleefully, and in a good mood, like he did every morning. He was the icon at the high-rise law firm called Bower at Law. Being the C.E.O. of the law firm was one thing to be proud of. But today, Eric Bower, a sixty-two-year-old six-foot-two-inch, 210-pound rich, white man was proud to wear an unusual happiness. At noon, the national news would be announcing his ten-million-dollar endorsement to Presidential Republican nominee Ben Scott's campaign. He was a firm believer in the Republican party, and hated the Democratic party with a passion. Eric saw all Democratic individuals as panhandlers who were destroying the American dream every day.

Today, I invested in a big difference, Eric thought as he walked to his office, simultaneously blowing the steam off his Maxwell coffee. He'd given all his employees a pleasant good morning. Now it was time to start his morning brief with his secretary, Londa Harris, in his office. *If I'm lucky, she'll probably give me a taste of her chocolate tits,* Eric thought of fucking Londa like he did every time he laid eyes on her. She was a gorgeous, extremely swarthy complexioned woman who'd recently graduated law school. She was working her last two weeks as Eric's secretary, before she started as a lawyer under his firm, like he'd promised her.

When Eric stepped into his office, the sight of the twin towers standing tall again made him feel at home. He sat his mug down on his Oakwood desk and walked up to the window, where he looked down at the busy streets, where pedestrians scrambled hastily to get to work. His office sat on the twenty-fourth floor of the high-rise building surrounded by unobstructed glass. It was always a beautiful sight for Eric every morning to see the city.

"I love this city," Eric said with his hands behind his back as he looked up into obscuring sky, promising a morning downpour at any moment.

"I'm sure the city loves you too, Mr. Bower" Londa said from behind Eric's desk. Eric smiled, always loving to hear Londa's sexy voice, and the redolence of her Rihanna performed.

"God, I hate to let you go woman, I'mma miss you voice every morning," Eric said as he turned around and looked Londa in her eyes as she sat in his plush chair in front of his desk with her legs crossed.

Her suit was like always, tight-fitting, accentuating her curves.

"Don't worry about losing me, I'll always be near and available, sir," Londa promised. "Good morning sir, um we're expecting company today. CBS news reporter Mike Biermann will be expecting an interview with you about your ten-million-dollar endorsement to the Republican candidate," Londa explained to Eric reading from her note's.

"That's great ..." Eric said, then took a sip from his coffee mug." What time during noon?"

"12:45 P.M. the vans will be pulling up, sir," Londa retorted as she flipped a page on her clipboard. "And we have a couple client visits also scheduled for today sir, starting at 2:30 P.M. with Mrs. Maslany," Londa informed Eric.

"Thank you so much, Londa ..." Eric said as he stood up out of his chair and walked over to a file cabinet. "I wouldn't know what to—"

Psst! Psst!

Eric head exploded from the two slugs that came crashing through the glass window. His brains and blood splattered on his desk and onto Londa's all white Chanel suit. Londa watched Eric body hit the floor, the stared at the two holes in the glass. When she looked beyond the two holes, she saw a woman on the next high rise aiming her rifle at her.

Oh, my God! Londa thought, making a run for it.

"Nooo! —"

Psst! Psst!

Before Londa could escape the threat, she was hit twice in her forehead and sat back down in her chair – lifeless.

Ayesha quickly broke down he rifle, and stored it back in her briefcase. She then removed her Glock 22 silencer from her waist, and walked into the bedroom where she had lovers tied up, sitting on the plush carpet.

"Please don't kill us, I swear we won't go to the authorities, lady," the boyfriend spoke in a husky voice.

"Sorry handsome, but you're already talking too much. If you were 'bout it than you wouldn't talk about it," Ayesha said, then aimed at the boyfriend's head.

Psst! Psst!! – Ayesha expected the girlfriend to scream, but she remained calm and appeared to be unafraid.

"So, you take heed, huh? That's how I learned the game, too," Ayesha said, then pulled the trigger twice, hitting the girlfriend in her head. Ayesha grabbed her belongings, and left the suite inconspicuously. When she got outside, she looked up at the sky and felt a light sprinkle. Ayesha merged into the pedestrian traffic, and hauled a cab

"The Hilton on Jefferson" Ayesha directed the Jamaican driver, while handing him $50 for the ride. "Keep the change."

"Thank you, mon," the Jamaican driver said smiling, revealing a toothless grill.

When Ayesha made it back to her hotel, she called her representative while sitting on the edge of the bed.

"Please enter your code name." – *Beep!* Ayesha quickly punched in her code name – Murderlicious.

"Thank you, please wait for our representative," the automated voice said to Ayesha, placing her on hold with Jazz music. A moment later, the line cleared.

"Job well done, Murderlicious. In twenty minutes, the same man will be to your door to pick up the tools," Ayesha's representative said, then hung up the phone. Ayesha sighed, then laid back on the bed with an evil smirk on her face.

"It's time. I feel that I am ready Master," Ayesha said amongst herself.

CHAPTER 6

"*B*en Scott, what is it that you have to tell CBS news about Mr. Bower, who invested ten million dollars to your campaign. Is his death connected to any motive of supporting you, sir?" the new reporter asked Ben Scott. He was being led by his security to the NYPD Headquarters to give a commiseration speech to the people of New York City, and to the families of philanthropist Constitutional Lawyer Eric Bower, and his secretary, Londa Harris.

"People, as the governor of New York, I express my sincere condolences for both individuals —"

"Girl, that creep probably got something to do with his murder. I don't trust his ass one bit," Alexis said to Ayesha and Tamara, who were sitting on the sofa in her living room.

Alexis was fed up with Ben Scott and all his supporters. She changed the channel, but saw the news conference on every channel. It was world Breaking News, and neither Alexis nor Tamara would have ever figured out that the killer was in their presence. They'd known their cousin to be a wild girl growing up, but never would they ever expect for her to harm a soul. The trio ate pizza and buffalo wings that were delivered while they watched the Breaking News – the only entertainment on TV.

When Ayesha showed up at Alexis' apartment by surprise, she'd just interrupted Alexis and her boyfriend, who were almost in their grooves. Alexis' boyfriend, Dave, was already in a rush and wanting a quickie before he went to work. But blood came first before pleasure any day in Alexis' world. Alexis called Tamara over and the trio popped a bottle of champagne and just talked about the old days.

"So Ayesha, who's the lucky man back home?" Tamara asked as she licked the buffalo sauce from her fingers.

"Why do he have to be a lucky guy? Plus, there's no one. I just pimp, fuck 'em, and release 'em," Ayesha said, reciting the lyrics to Young Zoe's hit "Player."

"So, you still breaking them clowns, huh?" Alexis chimed in.

"Yep, and a bitch banking –"

"Shit, what nigga money do you need," Tamara chimed in.

"All the money it takes to lay some good dick," Ayesha replied, causing both sisters to erupt into laughter.

"Ayesha, I swear the right niggas is gonna get yo' ass, and it's gonna be all over for you!" Alexis exclaimed.

"Well, thus far, they're all Mr. Wrongs, cousin," Ayesha retorted.

"So what, are we clubbing tonight or what?" Tamara asked,

"Shit, New York is y'all home bitch, lead the way," Ayesha retorted.

"I know what we could do –"

"What?!" Ayesha and Tamara asked in unison, anxious to hear what Alexis had to say. It was something that they did always throughout childhood, and hated when Alexis would withhold a thought or suggestion.

"I think we could go with Dave and his boy's to Legends tonight –"

"Who is his boys, and what the hell does Dave do? Last I checked Legends was where the ballers partied at," Ayesha interrupted Alexis.

"Bitch, you in heat?!" said then broke out with a chuckle.

"Whatever Alexis, you're the one coming to the club in heat."

"Yeah whatever, and Dave is a Fullback for the Buffalo Bills," Alexis said

"Why don't we see him in action?" Ayesha asked.

"Because he's not on the roster, he's on the practice squad until playoffs."

"So, they're saving the last for the show time, huh?" Ayesha asked.

"Yep," Alexis retorted.

Tamara rolled her eyes at Alexis' proud girl act, like she always did.

"Don't get too much of yourself," Tamara said.

"Don't hate, just don't be late," Alexis retorted.

"Do you have pictures of Dave's friends?" Ayesha asked, "Cause I ain't on the ugly duckling shit, Alexis."

"C'mere girl, look at his homeboy Craig," Alexis said as she strolled through her pictures in her iPhone.

Ayesha and Tamara both jumped from the sofa and stood over Alexis' shoulder as she sat in her La-Z-Boy chair.

"Damn, look at them abs!" Ayesha exclaimed, feeling the elegant man in the photo with Dave.

"That's Craig, and he's single," Alexis informed.

"Call him" Ayesha and Tamara exclaimed in unison.

"Back up bitch, I called him first," Ayesha warned Tamara.

"You got that, but I got sloppy seconds —"

"Ewww!" Ayesha and Alexis exclaimed in unison.

"What? It's good to keep dick in the family," Tamara exclaimed.

"I guess, I'm only looking for a good time —"

"Then y'all might as well give him a good time toge —"

"Don't even go there Alexis, I am not having a threesome with my claim cousin ... Grandma Elsa won't hear the last of it," Ayesha exclaimed.

"I'm only kidding ..." Alexis said laughing hysterically at the look on Ayesha and Tamara's faces.

"Well, it's not funny Alexis," Tamara said,

"She so nasty," said Ayesha, never taking her eyes off Craig.

* * *

DOWNTOWN MANHATTAN AT CLUB LEGENDS was like it was expected to be every Saturday night. Traffic was backed up and innumerable celebrities were in the enormous club having a good time. When Young Zoe and Boss' entourage walked through the doors, after stepping out of two stretch Hummer H2 limos, the fans in the club went wild. In his all black attire, Young Zoe's jewelry sparkled, catching eyes of many women in the club that were on their dates' arms nonchalantly, mesmerizing the young Philadelphia rapper. Young Zoe strutted over to the bar with Boss and looked around at the collection of different brands of alcohol,

"What we pissing out tonight, Boss?!" Young Zoe shouted over the Rihanna hit "Needed Me."

"Brown. Anything brown, son!"

"Now that's a Philly nigga for you," Young Zoe retorted.

"Baby, let me get five bottles of Remy Martin and keep them shit's coming on the hour. The top of the hour baby!" Young Zoe said to the sexy bartender who had an overbite grill and erect nipples, with a banging ass body.

"Okay Young Zoe, that'll be $500!" the sexy bartender retorted.

When Young Zoe grabbed the bottles, he purchased a side order of cups and a bag of ice. Him and Boss then moved with their entourage towards the VIP section. As they moved through the crowd, Young Zoe laid eyes on a chick he'd been trying to catch up with, and see what she was rating in bed. He name was Cherry, and she was the newest female rapper on the rise from Queens, NY. When he passed her, he winked his eye at her, and got a smile in return from her.

I'mma snatch that bitch before the night over with, Young Zoe promised himself.

He was glad to finally be out with Boss, and club with him. Doing concert's every other night in different cities gave them little time to interact with each other. Boss was his boy, and every time he got a chance, he would show his big homie his gratification for being a true friend.

"Bad bitches everywhere, Youngin'!" Boss shouted over the Lil' John hit.

"Turn down for what!" Young Zoe shouted back at Boss, sanging Lil' John's song with the hyped club. As they entered VIP together with their entourage. They ran into rappers and athletes from the NBA and NFL.

"I see Philly in the house tonight. One time for Young Zoe, who doing big things this year!" the DJ announced to the entire club. Young Zoe, accepting the acknowledgement and shout out, raised his bottle of Remy Martin in the air, with Boss.

"Yeah, us Philly nigga's in this bitch!" Young Zoe shouted, representing his city.

Ayesha was on the dance floor with Tamara and Alexis getting their groove on when they heard that Young Zoe was in the club. Ayesha never got a chance to see Young Zoe in person. But she'd always heard stories of him when she was growing up. People feared him, and he was once signed under her father's label. His pictures never gave he any recognition when she looked at them in magazines or on TV. *But he's appealing and extremely sexy,* Ayesha thought, as she broke her neck looking for Young Zoe.

"Girl, I want to go see that nigga!" Ayesha shouted to Alexis and Tamara over the music.

"Ayesha, you have a date and he's eye fucking the shit out of you!" Alexis shouted to Ayesha, then took a sip from her cup of Peach Cîroc.

When Ayesha looked back at the VIP booth, she indeed saw Craig eye fucking her. She gave him a faint smile, feeling herself blushing, then turned away from him. Craig was her package and she couldn't wait to get to a hotel room with him, to see how much manpower he really had. He was muscular and extremely handsome to Ayesha. *If he plays his cards right, Brandon might be out of luck,* Ayesha thought, then took a sip from her cup of Peach Cîroc. When she looked back at Craig, she saw him taking a swig from his bottle of Hennessy.

"I know he gonna fuck me all night. Alexis, that nigga taking it straight!" Ayesha said to Alexis.

"Girl, you better take it easy, and embrace yourself just in case he's a little too much for you —"

"Child, never that!" Tamara said,

"Look who's in our path!" Alexis pointed out. When Ayesha looked at the north of her, she met eyes with Young Zoe.

Oh my gosh, he's looking right at me! Ayesha thought as her heartbeat increased, and her palms became sweaty. *What the fuck is wrong with me and why is he looking at me like that?* Ayesha wanted to know.

"Are you okay, Ayesha? Damn, that nigga got you nutting on yo' self!" Tamara shouted, noticing the transformation in Ayesha.

When Ayesha turned away, she saw how her hands were trembling. She was completely surprised how her body was acting as well.

"It's this drink, got me trippin'!" Ayesha shouted.

When she looked back over at Young Zoe, he was making his way over to her with his entourage.

"Oh, shit we have company, and we have dates already —"

"And they're looking at us, too," Tamara chimed in when Young Zoe stepped in front of the trio. His eyes were on Ayesha, checking her out in her skin tight mini-dress, and leather for boot's.

"Do we know each other beautiful, because you sure do look familiar?!" Young Zoe asked Ayesha.

"Um... um..." she stuttered.

"We're from Philly as well!" Tamara helped Ayesha out.

"Damn, don't I know my kind? Huh, Boss?!"

"Never fails!" Boss consigned.

"So, what part of Philly, beautiful?"

"South Philly!" Ayesha retorted.

"Really?! What's yo' name ma and how come you stay in the –"

"Her name is Ayesha, and she got a nigga face to be in, homie!" Craig chimed in, stepping in with Dave and their boy Corey, who was Tamara's date.

Oh shit! Tamara thought.

"Wait a minute, don't no nigga own shit up in here, so let's get that straight!" Ayesha turned around, informing Craig with attitude.

"Bitch, who you think you talking too?!" Craig said.

Ayesha couldn't believe her ears. She knew, indeed, that Craig was drunk, and decided to let the disrespect slide. So, she laughed briefly, then looked him in his eyes.

"I'mma let that slide —"

"Man, a man ain't got no respect for his date lose out. Ma, all you have to say is the word, and we putting on for Philly in this bitch!" said Young Zoe.

"Naw'll he's a friend, he just had too much to drink. But, like I was saying, my name is Ayesha —"

Before Ayesha could finish giving her name to Young Zoe, she immersed quickly, and spun around to dodge Craig's attempt to grab her by her shoulders. She only had to read the look in Young Zoe's eyes. When she leaped back up to Craig's level, he had his arm in her hands so quick that her swiftness shocked everyone. With her drink on the ground, she was mad.

"Dave, I advise you to get yo' friend. He's had a little too much to drink!" Ayesha said to Dave as she held Craig's hand in a grip around his wrist.

"Dave get him, my cousin don't need this attitude!" Alexis shouted

"Bitch – uhh shit!" Craig screamed out in pain at the snap of his wrist,

"She broke my wrist, bro!"

"Nigga, get out my face before I break every bone in yo' body —"

Ayesha weaved the quick left Craig swung at her, and caught him by surprise with a nimble three piece to his face. Craig stumbled backwards and Ayesha followed up with a kick to his face, causing his nose to splatter in a gush of blood. Everyone, but Alexis and Tamara, stood in disbelief. They knew how good of a fighter their cousin was. But to Young Zoe and Boss, with their entourage, they all were stunned. When Craig hit the deck, Ayesha tried to finish him off, but was stopped short by two six-foot-five-inch, 250-pound bouncer's.

"What, you nigga's want some Philly beef, too?!" Ayesha shouted, challenging the bouncers who smiled ominously at Ayesha.

"Ma'am, we need you to leave the club, that's all!" one of the bouncers ordered.

"We will, come on Ayesha!" Alexis said then grabbed Ayesha by her arm and walked towards the exit.

Young Zoe stood and watched the beautiful Philly diva leave and couldn't explain to himself, why he didn't go after her. But if he wanted her, he had her name and knew that she was from South Philly.

"Boss, I want you to find out who she is, big bro. She bad son, and I mean bad!" Young Zoe shouted to Boss.

"I got you son!" Boss retorted

"Good, no let's turn this party out, my nigga!" Young Zoe said, then walked back towards VIP, where he found Cherry chatting with DMX.

Damn, that nigga done pulled my candidate! Young Zoe thought, as he passed by the duo. Young Zoe, being a man that women couldn't deny had stumbled across a set of model twins from Cuba. They were tipsy, and willing to take the party behind closed doors with Young Zoe and Boss. Young Zoe and Boss left Club Legend, with the twins and took them to Young Zoe's condo in Manhattan and partied until dawn came.

When Young Zoe arose at noon, the Cuban sisters were gone as well with Boss. Young Zoe walked downstairs to his bar and poured himself a glass of Remy Martin to work his hangover. Despite all the excitement he had with Boss and the twins. Sitting at his bar in his Polo briefs he only had one individual on his mind. – Ayesha! It was something more appealing about her, he just couldn't put it in words.

"I gotta find shorty," Young Zoe said, determinedly.

CHAPTER 7

$\mathcal{A}$yesha was back in Philadelphia at noon, enjoying the feeling of being back home. She had a wonderful time, despite having to check Craig. The most important matter was that she got to hang out with her cousins. Now, it was back to her normal life – anxious for her next call, so that she could transform into her girl, Murderlicious.

"Daddy, I wish you were here," Ayesha said, as she sat at her kitchen table and cleaned her favorite firearms, that were all Glock models. There were plenty times when she was alone, like now, that she'd sit and think of how impressive her father would be of her if he was alive.

"They never gave him a chance … he gave them what they wanted, and they still shot him," Ayesha said as silent tears cascaded down her face.

She was going into a surge of depression and felt the weight of the world on her shoulders. It's been awhile since she lost control of herself. The only person in the world that could calm her and make her see life in her control was her shrink. Ayesha wiped her tears then stood from the table with trembling hands and legs. She walked upstairs to her bedroom bathroom and rambled inside her medicine cabinet until she popped the top off the pill bottle and popped two capsules into her mouth. Ayesha turned on the water to the sink and swallowed a hand full of water, washing the pills down.

"I gotta find out who did this to my daddy ... it's the best I can do to show him my love and appreciation. What would he do if it was me?" Ayesha asked herself while staring in the mirror. "He would kill the bastard's entire family," Ayesha retorted with an impish smirk on her face.

* * *

BOSS WASTED no time investigating who Ayesha was. He agreed with Young Zoe that she looked very familiar, but he'd never seen her around. None of the men in his entourage had any clue of who she was, and had never seen her around, either. If there was one person that knew women well in the South Philly area, Boss knew that Bianca was his last hope. Ayesha didn't have a Facebook account, so he was at a dead end. And Google had too many Ayesha's to be certain he had the right one.

When Boss stepped out the back seat of the Lincoln Town Car, he pulled on his bear coat, then put on a pair of Gucci shades. He was summoned to meet with Bianca at an Italian restaurant in North Philly, a place he felt adamant of coming to due to being on his enemies' turf. But for Young Zoe, Boss was present to get the job done for Young Zoe. Coming prepared for a shout out was Boss' motto. He was far from vulnerability with his entourage of six men, ready to act on the slightest look of a threat. When Boss walked into the restaurant, eyes were all on him and his men. It was a laid-back restaurant, a place where Bianca had met many of her six-figure clients, and taken them back to her hotel room.

"May I help you, sir?" a red headed white waitress asked Boss as he approached the counter to check in.

"I'm Mr. Brown, and I have reservations for lunch," Boss responded.

"Yes, sir you do, um Bianca is waiting for you at the back table on aisle four, sir."

"Thank you, beautiful," Boss said, then quickly scanned the room for anything amiss. His wariness was evident to everyone in the area.

"Stay here y'all, I want be long," Boss ordered his men.

Boss walked into the dining area like he owned the place. The five-foot-ten-inch 245-pound turf lord had an ominous look that warned folks not to do anything to tick him off. Boss found Bianca sitting at a back table, eating a plate of spaghetti. The way her lips poked out as she sucked up a noodle made Boss' mind fluctuate to sexual desires of him and the high class Pimptress. Boss had always wondered what a night with Bianca would be like. But, unfortunate for him, Boss wasn't Bianca's type of me, not even with a million dollars. As Boss sat down, Bianca wiped sauce from her mouth with a napkin, then took a sip of her red wine.

"Sorry, if 'em late shorty —"

"No shorty here, Boss. Let's respect each other's profession for a good start, okay?" Bianca retorted in a feisty tone.

Boss hated bitches that got out of line, and had a reputation of putting them in their places. But Bianca feared nothing about Boss or his power. She had her own men who wouldn't hesitate to war it out with him. And that's why she chose North Philly, instead of South Philly. Her men were only one phone call away.

"I'll respect that, "B". Sorry if you feel insulted. It was never my intentions —"

"Let's get to business, Boss. I have business in a few minutes to get to," Bianca said, checking the time on her diamond Rolex.

"I need to know, do you know a woman name Ayesha from South Philly?" Boss asked getting to the punch.

"Do you have a picture of her?" Bianca asked.

"Naw'll … not at this moment," Boss admitted.

"There are a few Ayesha's I know, but how would I know whom it is you're inquiring about if I don't see how she is? This is a waste of time, Boss —"

"Listen, "B", stop with this sassy shit, okay. A nigga not none of your lame ass clients or hoes, so let's kill the attitude," Boss said to Bianca, who rolled her eyes at him. Boss was up to his neck with Bianca already, and wanted to reach across the table and grab her around her throat.

"Like I said, Boss, this is a blank mission. When you have a picture of her, just come see me. Until then, we have nothing further to say," Bianca said as she stood out her seat, simultaneously pulling her tight-fitting Vera Wang dress down.

Damn this bad bitch gets on my nerves! Boss thought.

"See you around Boss, come better prepared," Bianca said, then walked away from the table, leaving Boss sitting down. Boss watched Bianca's ass jiggle all the way to the front counter. He liked everything about Bianca but her fuckin' attitude.

"I'mma put a stop to her fly mouth," Boss said to himself the stood to depart the restaurant as well.

Boss had no clue of how he would get a photo of Ayesha to produce to Bianca. But he had a plan that would get him closer to Ayesha, and get some information on her. *She's from South Philly – someone knows who she is,* Boss thought. The women a better option came to his mind.

"Bingo! Yo' Chris, drive over to 120th and Jenkins," Boss ordered his driver.

"Yes, sir Boss."

If there was no way to find out a person's identity from the streets, then that's when an expert job becomes reliable, Boss thought as he sparked flame to his hydro blunt.

* * *

"So, do you think that you may just be in too much anger that's causing you your sudden grief?" the Master asked Ayesha, who was relaxing on a sofa in a reclining position in front of Mr. King's desk. It'd been awhile since Ayesha did an evaluation in Mr. King's office rather than sparring her frustration away. With her eyes closed, Ayesha answered the Master.

"I'm just tired of not knowing, sir," Ayesha purred, trying her best to control her emotions. *But it's hard for her, and would probably be for any female in her predicament,* Mr. King thought.

"Ayesha ... if you react off pain, that will be dangerous for you," Mr. King said as he removed his glasses from his face and folded his hands together.

"You have to think like the professional you are, Murderlicious. Because the moment you don't, it could affect a lot of people," Mr. King informed Ayesha concisely.

Ayesha knew that the Master was a powerful man, she just didn't know to what degree and what profession. If she'd known that he had ties to the CIA, Ayesha would've become enlighten on her victims' reasons of being dead. She had no clue that for the last couple months, she'd been working for the CIA and why they chose her to handle their problems. It was Mr. King's credit of making Ayesha the killing machine she was today.

"Mr. King ..." Ayesha spoke as she raised up and looked the Master in his eyes.

"I wouldn't do nothing to risk no one's life that matters to me. But I am tired of waiting for a clue to drop in my lap. Someone knows something and I need to hear it," Ayesha explained.

"Come with me, Ayesha," Mr. King said as he stood out his seat. Ayesha watched Mr. King walk towards the door of his office, then followed him. She trailed Mr. King through the hall in his opulent home and entered a room full of file cabinets.

"Close the door," he ordered without looking back, and as he walked to a file cabinet. Ayesha closed the door and locked it for better precaution. When she turned around, Mr. King had a thick file in his hand that he'd pulled from a file cabinet.

"Yours" he said as he handed the file over to Ayesha.

"This is everything you need to get you started. Just promise me something —"

"What is it?" Ayesha asked.

"Promise me that you will be careful when you begin your process of elimination?" Mr. King asked. Ayesha knew exactly what he meant by process of elimination, and to know that much, she knew that the file in her hand contained some valuable information.

"I promise you that I will be careful, Mr. King," Ayesha gave her word.

"Good, now let's remember that you are still on call. Finding the killer in your father's murder is important, but your loyalty to your profession is also," Mr. King advised Ayesha.

"Mr. King, can I ask you a question?"

"Go ahead, young lady."

"Will you ever tell me who I am looking for?"

The question didn't take Mr. King by surprise at all. He knew that her curiosity would get the best of her. But unfortunately for Ayesha, Mr. King had to respect the code of silence, just like her.

"If I ever tell you, it won't even be on my dying bed, Murderlicious. All I can tell you is that you were referred to the same superiors I once had, by me," Mr. King said as he placed a hand on Ayesha's shoulder and gave it a squeeze.

"Just know that you are a powerful woman, and when the time do come for you to learn everything, trust me, you will know," Mr. King said, then winked his eye at Ayesha.

"Thanks."

"You're welcome. Now, let's go watch our girl, Sarah Krakowski, kick some ass," Mr. King said then led Ayesha to his living room, where they were just on time to see Sarah step into the ring.

"You're still adamant about giving the UFC a try, huh?" Mr. King asked Ayesha as they watched Sarah display her gold champion belt to her rowdy fans.

"It's just not for me, sir."

"Maybe you feel like you'll lose going for the title, is that what it is?" Mr. King pressed on.

"Nope … it's just not thrilling like killing is," Ayesha responded.

"I'll agree. I once wore my code name above everything else, too."

"There she goes" Ayesha said as she watched Sarah square off with her opponent from Asia. Ayesha and Mr. King watched the fight, like the world, last for thirty minutes before Sarah won by a TKO kick to the Asian girl's jaw.

I told you that you would win, Ayesha thought.

"That fight just made her $250,000, win or lose Ayesha ... you still don't —"

"Nope ... it's not for me sir," Ayesha retorted.

* * *

IT WAS an hour before Boss had met with his boy Bruce Hines, who was the best P.I. (Private Investigator) in the area. Bruce was in an important meeting with other P.I.'s, and recommended for Boss to wait for him in his office. Boss was grateful for Bruce's secretary Tonya, who accommodated all his needs while he waited.

"So, tell me homie what brings you to the P.I.'s office?" Bruce asked as he removed his Philadelphia Eagles cap from his head and rubbed his head. Boss sat in a comfortable leather chair in front of Bruce's desk full of paperwork and files.

"I need a favor, Bruce ... and you're my last result," Boss replied, while pulling on his goatee.

"I can't say no favors to you, Boss. Shit, you're the reason I'm still alive son," Bruce reminded Boss of his close call to death a few years ago, when Boss came out of nowhere and shot to death two North Philly niggas who were jacking Bruce in South Philly, at a Wawa gas station.

"Well, if that's a yes, son, I need your help locating a female from South Philly."

"What's her name?" Bruce asked as he fired up his data on his desk computer.

"Her name is Ayesha," Boss replied. "I only have a first name," Boss added as Bruce typed in Ayesha as his target name for the South Philly area.

"My data is pulling up five Ayesha's from the South Philly area, and they're all in the age range of 18-28 years old —"

"Do you have any photos of them?" Boss asked.

"Let me see," Bruce said as he tapped his mouse twice.

"There's only two showing up, and that's because the others have no criminal record, if that helps you in any kind of way —"

"Let me see the two you have," Boss asked as he got out of his seat, and came around Bruce's desk to look at the computer screen. When Boss looked at the two mug shots, he saw that neither women were the Ayesha that he was looking for.

"Where's the other three at?" Boss asked

"They're two clicks backwards ..." Bruce said as he clicked the mouse twice, bringing the previous page to display.

"Ayesha C. Smith, she's 28 years old, Ayesha D. Morris, she's 25 years old, and Ayesha T. Jordan, she's 18 years old. That's all from the South Philly area, I'm guessing when you looked that you get national, huh?" Bruce asked Boss.

"Exactly Bruce. I need the photos of them last three Ayesha's, son."

"Okay, as a favor, I gotta give you the full discount —"

"What the fuck you mean, nigga. I saved yo' life and didn't charge you shit!" Boss exploded.

"You're forgetting I was hustling for you before I found my job, Boss. We cool, but I'm in a business. Look at my desk, all these files are prepaid. So, for me to put any of them aside to accommodate you, Boss is flat out depriving my clients of a thoroughly well job of my profession." Bruce explained.

Boss understood Bruce's principle, and had no choice but to respect it. Bruce was right in every aspect. It didn't matter how close his life was almost over with a few years ago. Bruce had the favor, and he was still on the clock.

"How much on the discount?" Boss asked,

"For you, Boss, $1,200, and I'll have these women's photos by the end of the week," Bruce promised.

"Is this a promise?"

"I promise you, I will have them by the end of the week," Bruce assured Boss, who knew that Bruce was the man to count on. *I wouldn't have wasted my time, if I couldn't count on him,* Boss thought,

"$1,200?" Boss asked,

"$1,200," Bruce retorted,

"What's the original price?" Boss asked to see how he was on the discount. Instead of telling Boss, Bruce exited the program and entered a data of prices for every individual search.

"Price of one individual search local is $5,000. If they're out of state $10,000 and the price tag goes on as you see," Bruce said, giving Boss a tour of the prices for innumerable means of requesting a P.I.'s expertise.

Boss, after seeing with his own eyes that Bruce wasn't trying to pull one over on him, dug in his pockets and retrieved a hefty wad of straight hundreds. Bruce's estimated the wad of cash to be more than $10,000 as he watched Boss peel off $1,200.

"You have my number…" Boss said as he handed the money to Bruce. "I'll be waiting on yo' call, son," Boss retorted, then walked towards the door of Bruce's office.

"Boss," Bruce called out, before Boss could open the door.

Boss turned around and said, "What is it?"

"How much is that coat?"

"Not for sale son," Boss replied, "A lot of blood homie, that's all I could tell you," Boss replied, then exited Bruce's office.

A lot of blood huh? Bruce thought, then got to work.

CHAPTER 8

*A*yesha had finally got a chance to sit down with the file that Mr. King had given her after a shower and feeding herself a TV dinner. She was now sitting at the table in her kitchen after midnight bracing herself for whatever laid before her in the file of her father.

What am I expecting? Ayesha thought then sighed as she opened the file. Ayesha's heart dropped when she saw a mugshot photo of her father. He was younger than she'd ever seen him. He was nowhere near the age of forty in the photo. He had to be no more than twenty.

"Daddy, help me out here," Ayesha said, then began her examination of the file.

For the first five minute's, Ayesha had no clue of what she was looking at. It wasn't until she saw the Philadelphia police department investigation log that she realized that she was reviewing her father's cold case file. Ayesha had access to every witness that was interviewed in the investigation. Every anonymous interview was in the file, and the potential suspects that the Philadelphia police had to let go because of corroborated alibi's. The two detectives that had given up on Tommy Vantrell Jordan's murder were the first two people that Ayesha would pay a visit to. It was time for her to get some answers and direction for her daddy murder. And she was closer than she had ever been in ten long years. She couldn't think Mr. King enough for revealing the file to her.

"This is cause for a celebration; don't you think so, Ms. Murderlicious?" Ayesha stated as she closed the file and picked up her cordless phone. She dialed a number she knew off her head and waited for the party to answer.

"Hello"

"What's up?" Ayesha asked seductively,

"I'm in your back yard … What's up with you?" Brandon asked.

"How far could you get to my back door?" Ayesha asked as she nibbled on her index finger nail.

"Shit, give me five minutes, baby," Brandon retorted,

"Four minutes … I'll be waiting," Ayesha retorted, then hung up the phone.

She was already in her satin robe with just a pair of black thongs on, and highly horny. That's when Ayesha knew that her next kill was only hours away. It was like her body knew when it wanted to be Murderlicious and Ayesha. Four minutes flat, and Brandon was knocking at the front door. Ayesha strutted from the kitchen and went to open the front door for Brandon. When she opened the door, and saw Brandon, who stood six-foot-one-inches, 175 pounds in a black wife beater, accentuating his muscular frame. She almost nutted on herself. His peanut butter skin was flawless, and his Jordan cologne was a complete turn on.

"Did someone call for a lift?" Brandon asked as he stepped in closer to Ayesha and lifted her chin. While looking down at her searching her eye's. But, like always, he could never figure the gorgeous woman out, and why she was avoiding a committed relationship with him.

"Why you looking like you'd rather leave me on the side of the road?" Ayesha asked, biting on her bottom lip.

"Woman, you're too beautiful to even think about leaving you alone … remember, when you ready for the official, daddi is ready," Brandon said then kissed Ayesha on her lips softly.

Ayesha wrapped her arms around Brandon's neck and intensified the kiss as he lifted her off her feet.

"Fuck me, Brandon … that's all I want you to do!" Ayesha purred.

Brandon walked inside the condo and closed the door, shut with his foot. He carried Ayesha over to the plush sofa and laid her on her back. Ayesha slipped out of her robe as she watched Brandon strip out of his clothes and slide a condom onto his enormous, erect dick. Ayesha rolled over and positioned her ass in the air in the doggy style position and waited for Brandon to enter her wet pussy. Brandon removed Ayesha's thong quickly.

"Fuck me, Brandon," she ordered, then immediately felt Brandon sinking into her world slowly. Brandon held onto Ayesha's waist as he sank his nine inches inside of her. With an arched back, Ayesha gasped for air as Brandon thrusted in and out of her pussy.

"Oh, Brandon, fuck me!"

Brandon grabbed a hand full of Ayesha's long, straight ironed hair and pulled it like she loved it.

"Yes, baby fuck … me har—der!" Ayesha demanded as she began to throw her pussy back at Brandon.

Brandon loved when his bitches took his dick like a pro, especially when they had tight pussy like Ayesha. She was blowing his mind, and every time he fucked her, he was only falling more hooked on her. She was the best of his collection, and he was ready to drop every female just to have her. *But like Drake and Rihanna, commitment is far from her plans,* Brandon thought as he pumped in and out of Ayesha's pussy. He fucked her like it was his last pussy on earth, and met all her demands. Communing was all it would ever be between them, Brandon was just hoping that a change of heart would occur for Ayesha. Because beautiful as she was, and low key, she was every man's trophy. He had no clue that beyond her beauty was a world so dark as night and vast that he would never understand.

"I'm … cumming, Brandon!" Ayesha moaned out loud as she came to an electrifying orgasm. In three stokes, Brandon came himself, exploding inside the condom. *Damnit!*

* * *

HE WAS CLASSIFIED AS A TERMINATOR, and was ordered to carry out an extirpation mission for the CIA. The incognito stood six-foot-two-inches, 210 pounds, and was an artistic martial arts black belt at thirty-six years old. Like every other hire for murder, he was eager to take his target out. He knew everything about his target and had come prepared for a battle if his target refused to comply. The incognito stepped out of his black SUV, in all-black attire with a hoodie jacket on, and a pair of sun shades. He walked a block down from the park he'd parked at, and came upon his target's residence.

It was 3 o'clock a.m. and the Incognito had no intentions of knocking on the door. He walked around to the side of the house, and found the small box next to the meter that controlled the house alarm. From his back pocket, he removed a flat head screwdriver and quickly removed four screws from the box. When the box was open, the Incognito had access to a bundle of wires. He placed the flat head screw driver back into his back pocket, then dug in his needle nose pliers. He flicked the lighter to illuminate the dark confines of the box. The Incognito found the red and green wire and clipped them, disconnecting a transfer of power. Satisfied with his disengagement of the alarm system, he moved to the back yard.

The Incognito found the back sliding door and picked the lock with a special custom-made key that allowed him to pull the entire lock pad out once inserted in the grooves of the lock. The Incognito slid back the sliding door and entered the kitchen. For a moment, he listened to the sounds of the luxury home. He heard a distant TV on upstairs and the soft sound of Jazz music playing. The Incognito pulled out his .9mm silencer, the strutted through the darkness towards the flight of stairs. When he made it to the stairs he took them light footed and with extra precaution. When the Incognito made it to the top of the stairs, he was taken by surprise when his target kicked the gun out his hand and kicked him in his stomach.

The Incognito stumbled backwards, falling down the stairs with his gun. It was dark as hell, and his target had advanced on him. *Shit!* The Incognito thought as he hit the bottom of the stairs.

His target was on him in no time, the Incognito saw his silhouette and gave his target a kick to his groin, simultaneously leaping up from the ground. Hearing his target groan let him know that he'd had kicked the wind out of them. But as the Incognito tried grabbing his target, his target chopped him with his hands in his knees and brought him down to one knee. The target tried punching the Incognito in his face, but the Incognito read his target's intention, and caught his wrist, ending his target's strength with a quick snap.

"Aww shit!" the target screamed in pain.

The Incognito then gave his target's arm a snap, breaking his arm from the shoulder down. The Incognito's target hit the deck, moaning in pain. He walked away from his target, and flicked on a light. When he saw his target, who was now feeble, the Incognito smiled impishly. He espied his gun by the foot of his target and walked towards it to pick it up. As he leaned down to pick up the gun, his target attempted to deliver a defensive kick, but was too feeble. The Incognito grabbed his target's leg and snapped it like he'd done his arm.

"Lord, why?!" his target cried out.

"Because sir ..." the Incognito said, breathless as he retrieved his gun. "You have to die," he said as he aimed at the Master's head.

"Who ... sent you?!" the Master asked, panting.

"You know who sent me sir, I think they gave you a chance to avoid this by leaving the country, sir. By the way, I was told to tell you that the head man said thanks for Murderlicious. She's proving to be the best female ever."

"Tell her that I love her —"

Psst! Psst! Psst! Psst!

"I will sir," the Incognito promised, after shooting the Master four times in his face and forehead. The Incognito left the Master's luxury home without anyone ever seeing him. The Master was his fourth legendary assassination that he'd carried out in one year. And they all were somewhat connected to the CIA

* * *

As the sun seeped through her drapes, Ayesha felt like a big day was promised for her. Her and Brandon had a splendid time together last night. She could still smell his Jordan cologne redolently in her bedroom. After their first round of hard core fucking, Brandon had carried Ayesha to her bedroom, and slow stroked her all throughout the wee hours. Brandon was only an hour behind the first sighting of dawn. Ayesha was far from sleep. The file of her father was all that was on her mind.

Ayesha arose from bed nude, and walked insider her bathroom. She took a morning piss, then hopped inside a hot steaming shower. Ayesha grabbed a two-blade razor and began shaving her plump mound completely bald. She then shaved her legs and arms thoroughly. Satisfied, she scrubbed her body clean with "OGX" argon oil and Morocco body wash, then washed her hair thoroughly. When Ayesha stepped out the shower, she wrapped her head in a towel bun, then dried her body with another towel as she walked into her bedroom.

She felt like a new woman on a mission of her life. She couldn't tell you if it was because of the good fucking that Brandon had laid down, or her eagerness to begin her hunt for her father's killing. Ayesha slid on a pair of silk thongs, then slid into a lustrous mini Jason Wu dress and some Jason Wu heels. She strapped on a thigh gun holster and secured her .380. Ayesha braided her hair in a long Indian braid, then threw on a Philadelphia Eagles cap to match her outfit. As Ayesha walked down stairs, she heard her Verizon Track Phone ringing.

"Shit!" Ayesha exclaimed at the call coming at the wrong time. She reached into her purse and dug out her phone.

"Hello"

"Please enter your code name." – *Beep!* Ayesha quickly entered her code name – Murderlicious.

"Thank you, please wait for your representative," the automated voice said to Ayesha then put her on hold, with Jazz music. A moment later, the line cleared and Ayesha heard her representative.

"Murderlicious?"

"Yes sir, this is me," Ayesha retorted.

"Jersey City, New Jersey 1202 110th and Texas Street. His name is Mr. Stephen O'Brien. He is to be extirpated," Ayesha's representative said, then hung up the phone.

"Damnit!" Ayesha exclaimed then looked at what she had on.

"I'm not fit for a kill ... fuck it, I'll change when I get to Jersey," Ayesha said, then proceeded back upstairs, where she packed her necessary gear in a duffel bag. When she came back downstairs, she grabbed her father's file off of the kitchen table, then left her condo. When she got into her all black .745, she played her favorite song by Rihanna, "Needed Me."

"That girl is doing her thang this year, for real," Ayesha stated as she pulled out of her condo complex.

* * *

DETECTIVE MATTHEW CRANMER and his partner Christina Lindsey were the toughest detectives in Philadelphia, making a hundred arrests a year on murder suspects. In spite of the large number of successful arrests, the statistics to cold cases filed were vast. When the duo pulled up to the crime scene of their first homicide of the day, crime scene veterans were everywhere trying to find anything that could be evidence. Detective Cranmer's six-foot-five height didn't bother to immersed underneath the yellow tape like Lindsey did, who stood five-foot-five-inches, 145 pounds, and was a Jennifer Aniston look alike. Both detectives were in their late forties and had an honest dedication to their jobs. They took it personal and felt indebted to the families who lost their love ones.

"Who would want the Psychotherapist dead?" Lindsey asked Cranmer as they walked through the front door.

"Who knows ... could be some ill patient of his," Cranmer considered.

"That's a good start. Let's see what Carie has to say," Lindsey retorted as a (CSI) approached her, who both detectives were closely acquainted with.

"Hey Carie" Cranmer spoke while putting on a pair of gloves.

"It's an enigma this far. His house keeper is the one who discovered him. When she stepped inside, she found him at the foot of the stairs," Carie explained while pointing at Mr. Bernard King underneath a white shroud. Carie was a cute blonde good at her work.

"Where is she at?" Lindsey asked Carie.

"She's down at the precinct being interviewed."

"Let's take a look," Cranmer said, then walked over to Mr. King's body, squatted down, and pulled back the head of the shroud. The nature of the wounds always told a story for Cranmer. And what he saw was gruesome and a hit that was meant for no survivors.

"Broken arm, and leg is evident, I'd say," Cranmer said.

"Yeah, but it's not the cause of death," Lindsey retorted.

"Do we have any neighbors that seen anything amiss?" Cranmer asked. Carie shook her head – no.

"Great" Cranmer said as he stood back up.

CHAPTER 9

$\mathcal{A}$yesha had made it to Jersey City, New Jersey by noon and laid low in a nearby hotel. She was waiting for the sun to go down so that she could slip off into the night. Sitting Indian style on the queen-sized bed, Ayesha had her father file open and had been attentive, getting familiar with the contents of the file for the last two hours since she'd arrived at the hotel. She had no clue what was occurring back home in Philadelphia. When she was on a mission, she was strictly disengaged from the world until she was done. Ayesha was now learning about the prostitution ring her father regulated from 54th Street to 61st and how much money he was bringing in from the operation.

"Damn dad, you had a damn gold mine two ways. The studio, and the prostitution ring," Ayesha said as she read through the FBI information. She read the report thoroughly and there was an unfulfilled gap somewhere in the investigation that she noticed.

Why the fuck the Pimptress, Ariel, wasn't ever questioned about the murder, and her whereabouts? Ayesha asked herself, and made a mental note to ask Mr. King about her and what he thought about Ariel. Ayesha looked at the potential suspect's and saw that they were all from North Philly. It was clear to her that for many generations,

North Philly and South Philly were rivals. But nobody seemed to believe that Tommy Gun had let his enemies from another turf run down on him. *And all the potential suspects had alibis,* Ayesha thought. Her gut feeling was telling her that the enemy was very close and that they were closer than Quavis.

"It was definitely a hit, dad. So tell me, where is your killer?" Ayesha asked the papers in front of her hoping that a clue would pop out. *Why would I want you dead, and kill you in front of your daughter?* Ayesha thought.

"Someone wanted the streets out of your control, daddy," Ayesha said, then flipped through more papers in the file.

"Someone knows something," Ayesha said.

She couldn't call up none of her ex-boyfriends that used to tell her about her daddy, because they were all doing time in prison or dead after being gunned down in the streets. She could remember her first boyfriend, who'd taken her virginity at fourteen years old. His name was K-Dawg and he was twice her age, considered a small-time hustler. He used to tell her how her father had a lot of respect in the streets and had a lot of nigga's in fear. "South Philly lost a legendary when Tommy Gun was killed."

K-Dawg was killed a couple months before she'd turned fifteen years old. She was so full of anger that she had no clue how to go about finding the killer. Her mind was complacent on the fact that if the police couldn't find the killer, then there was no way that she would find the killer, either. She had a different mindset today. She just had to find the people who could explain.

"Don't worry daddy, we will find them," Ayesha said, then closed her eyes to meditate on the situation she had at hand.

* * *

(INSERT MUSIC NOTE) "Never gave two shits about South Philly son/my burner be known to let y'all feel summer/who you? Young ho'/Nigga yo' ass get smoke like Altimo / this Breezy Young Zoe give me a reason / I got pull like Tommy Gun / Haiti boy yo deaf? /12th

and Hunt-em-down, that's Huntingdon son click clack bang/" (insert music note)

Murder-"

Young Zoe had enough of hearing the dis track that was aimed directly at him from another underground rapper named Breezy, who was from North Philly.

"Yo son, that nigga gotta be high to put that shit out like that," Boss said to Young Zoe, who was sitting on Boss' plush sofa at his baby mansion, on the out skirts of South Philly.

"This nigga is dead son, I'mma teach him how to cook some real beef. I see he still pulling on a dead man's balls," Young Zoe replied.

"Man, that nigga ain't worth them crackers coming at you, son ... let the Boss handle business," Boss said. Young Zoe took a sip from his cup of Remy Martin straight without any chaser, then looked at Boss.

"I'mma drop a hit ... and I'mma call it "Hot 72" Boss. I want this nigga lights out in the next 72 hours' son," Young Zoe ordered.

"I got you, son."

"I know you do, now let's go drop this hit," Young Zoe said as he stood up and prepared to leave Boss' baby mansion.

"Aye, Boss?" Young Zoe called out when he made it to the front door.

"What's good, son?"

"I been thinking 'bout that bad bitch we met in the club. It's just something about her that got me on some love boy shit."

"I don't know, she do look like if a nigga do get with her, a nigga gotta be 'bout their business. But let's not give her high standards, she might be just like the rest of these hoes in South Philly —"

"Then why is it we don't know her? That bitch is a house girl that don't play when it comes to strapping," said Young Zoe.

"My boy Bruce will have us some positive news by the weekend," Boss said.

"Alright, well let me go handle this track, you handle that nigga, and I want anybody in his vicinity, hit up," Young Zoe ordered Boss.

"I got you, son," Boss retorted.

When Young Zoe was in the back seat to the Hummer H2 limo,

Mac pulled off from Boss' mansion. His mind went back to Ayesha. For a woman, she knew how to hold herself down. That shit was a big turn on for Young Zoe. He was a good brawler, but the martial arts was a different field for him. It was brawl or shout it out with his foe's, and these day's there were less brawls and excessive shouting's. Young Zoe thought.

"Yo' Mac, what do you think about this nigga Breezy?" Young Zoe asked his driver, who he knew had heard the dis track like the entire Philadelphia and the world.

"I think he's a fool to be barking up the wrong tree," Mac retorted, as he made a left turn. "You do plan on responding back, right?" Mac asked.

"Yeah ... it's called "Hot 72" for his ass. I'mma release 72 bars of pressure, then fill the boy body with 72 slugs," Young Zoe informed Mac.

"Sounds like a good plan," Mac retorted, smiling.

* * *

Mr. Stephen O'Brien was a powerful man in Jersey City, New Jersey. He was the voice of the commission board and an endorsing Republican that had recently endowed two million dollars to Ben Scott's campaign. Tonight, he'd celebrated with his wife at dinner at an expensive restaurant in downtown Jersey City. Mr. O'Brien felt like he was making a difference for his country by coming forth with his endowment for Governor Presidential nominee Ben Scott. Mr. O'Brien hated the Democrats, despite his act on helping the low-class community. He only gave the blacks proposals rather than committing to their neighborhood.

Ben Scott is a man that will change the Democratic laws and make it hell for the complacent low-class living folks, Mr. O'Brien thought as he stepped out of the hot steaming shower. At fifty-seven years old, the old man had enough of the colored folk's laziness. *They're running a well dry with fuckin' handouts,* Mr. O'Brien thought as he dried off. His wife Susan was in the bedroom ending her night early so that she could report to work in the early a.m. Mr. O'Brien was lucky that he got a chance to make love to her tonight.

"She wasn't like Kate, but it would do until I get to her," Mr. O'Brien said to himself speaking of the underage girl he had been dealing with sexually on an everyday basis.

Mr. O'Brien put on a pair of old, loose fitting underwear, then walked into his and his wife's bedroom. The TV was on, illuminating the darkness in the room. When he looked at the bed, he saw that Susan had the covers over her head. *Now she knows that's not safe when she already has breathing problems,* Mr. O'Brien thought as he shook his head and walked around to his side of the bed. He climbed in bed and pulled the covers from over his wife's face.

"Oh, my Lord!" Mr. O'Brien shouted as he stared at a motionless Susan, whose throat was cut from ear to ear, with blood soaking the sheets. Mr. O'Brien's heart was beating rapidly as his body went into shock. When he looked up into the doorway he saw the silhouette of an intruder walking into the room. When the intruder got into eye sight, he saw that it was a woman who held a gun in her hand. She aimed at him with an impish smirk on her face.

"Hello Mr. O'Brien, how was your day?" Ayesha asked a timorous Mr. O'Brien, who was speechless and appeared to be going into a heart attack.

"Nope! You gotta die this way, sir," Ayesha said, then squeezed the trigger, catching Mr. O'Brien between his eyes.

Psst! Psst! Psst! Psst!

Ayesha emptied the clip on Mr. O'Brien body, then left his residence inconspicuously. Her job was completed in Jersey City, New Jersey, and a journey awaited her back in Philadelphia. When Ayesha returned to her hotel to gather her belongings, her Verizon track phone rung.

"Hello"

"Please enter your code name." *–Beep!*

Ayesha quickly entered her code name – Murderlicious.

"Thank you, please wait for your representative," the automated voice informed Ayesha followed by Jazz music. A moment went by before the line cleared.

"Murderlicious?"

"Yes sir, it's me."

"Good job, you may return, but stay on call," her representative said, then hung up the phone.

"Back to Philly," Ayesha said as she grabbed her duffel bag and stormed out the hotel, leaving no trace of evidence behind her.

CHAPTER 10

*A*yesha couldn't believe that North Philly rapper Breezy had released a dis track on Young Zoe. The fact that he'd mentioned her father's name in his track had her upset. She wished that she could see Breezy face to face to tell him how she felt about it.

"I wish motherfuckers would just leave my dad alone," Ayesha said as she came to a red light at an intersection in South Philly. As she waited for the light to turn green, she listened to the radio host speak on the opinions of the dis track from people who were calling in. The track had a lot of Young Zoe fans wondering what his reply would be, including Ayesha herself.

"I think he's gonna come back and hold South Philly down," a fan who'd called in to the radio station said.

When the light turned green, Ayesha pulled off with the traffic as one of Young Zoe's song was being played. Ayesha loved the song and turned up the volume. It made her think about the night she encountered Young Zoe at Club Legend in Manhattan, NY. *I would have never expected for me to react the way I did when I seen him. The look in his eyes was lust. I'd never had a man just kill me with his eyes. I can only imagine what his fuck game would do,* Ayesha thought as she pulled into her condo complex.

It was 2:30 a.m. and the complex was quiet like any other wee hour occasion. Ayesha killed the engine and grabbed her duffel bag. When she stepped out of the car, headlights swept into the complex and came towards her complex. When the SUV pulled her .745 she became alert and reached for her .380 from her thigh holster. The doors open and two plain clothes detectives stepped out. *What the hell do they want?* Ayesha thought, as they walked up to her with extreme precautions, and their guns drawn.

"Ma'am, is that a weapon in your hands?" Detective Lindsey asked Ayesha.

"What the fuck do you think it is, who the hell are you two?"

"Ma'am, we're detectives with the Philadelphia police department. We only want to ask you a couple questions, ma'am. Could you please put the gun away," Lindsey asked nicely.

Ayesha sighed a breath of relief, she was grateful for the police to be a replacement of any threat. She complied and returned her gun to her thigh holster. When both detectives saw no threat in Ayesha, to start good rapport, they returned their weapons to their holsters on their waist.

"What's going on?" Ayesha asked as she leaned up against her car, folding her arms with her duffel bag in her hand.

"Ma'am, when was the last time you visited your psychotherapist Mr. Bernard King?" Detective Cranmer asked.

"Yesterday afternoon, we watched the UFC fight together … Why??" Ayesha asked, becoming alarmed. But as quick as it came it diminished, when she thought about how well Mr. King could hold his own. He was the man who'd taught her everything she knew today.

"Ma'am …" Cranmer said, then cleared his throat.

"Sometime yesterday around midnight, someone broke into Mr. Kings home and killed him in cold blood. Do-"

"What are you telling me, sir … someone killed Mr. King?" Ayesha asked as she raised up off her car.

"Sadly, to say ma'am, yes. He was murdered and we're investigating."

Ayesha wasn't hearing shit that Cranmer was saying. A big hole had impacted her chest and it was painful. She had no clue that tears were falling from her eyes. Neither did she realize that her body was trembling badly.

"Ma'am, are you okay?" Lindsey asked.

Ayesha looked at Detective Lindsey with an impish look on her face, unaware of it herself. Ayesha wanted to take on the world and kill every person involved of killing Mr. King.

"He was a dad to me, please let me see him," Ayesha asked Cranmer and Lindsey.

Both detectives looked at each other and had the same prospect in their minds about Ayesha. Despite the investigation being in its early stage and everyone having to be treated like a suspect. Both detectives knew that Ayesha wasn't a suspect. The pain she was showing was the signs of a victim, and both equipped detectives were sharing that same prospect. But it was impossible for them to pull Ayesha into a funeral home without drawing attention and breaking their policy.

"Please let me see him," Ayesha protested after seeing that both detectives were adamant.

"Ma'am we can't —"

"Come with us Ayesha, but promise to give us an alibi when we're done," Cranmer chimed in, taking control of the situation. He didn't know why he was willing to break the policy, but he felt that he was doing the right thing. He knew all about Ayesha losing her father and he'd heard her cry when she said that Mr. King was a father to her.

"I will, sir … I was home at midnight my friend and phone records could vouch for me," Ayesha said.

"Do you have a permit for that gun, Ayesha?" Lindsey asked.

"Yes, I do. If I didn't, then I wouldn't have it," Ayesha retorted, with attitude.

"Come … I'm going over my head with this one, so let's be quick about this, Ayesha," Cranmer said, then walked off towards the unmarked SUV. As he took the wheel, Ayesha hopped inside the back seat while Lindsey took her seat up front on the passenger side. *First my dad … and now the man who's taught me everything. What is going on?*

Ayesha thought on the edge of breaking down, but she managed to keep herself intact.

Twenty minutes later, Cranmer pulled into the Yate's Funeral home ran by a family that migrated from Florida. He pulled around back and parked behind a black hearse.

"Give me couple minutes you two, sit tight," Cranmer said, then exited the SUV.

Lindsey and Ayesha watched Cranmer walk up to the back door of the funeral home and knock a couple times. A moment later, the door came open and Cranmer said a few words before he stepped inside and closed the door. *What is he doing?* Lindsey thought. The silence in the SUV was eerie and Lindsey felt obligated to spark up a conservation.

"Ayesha ... do you know of anyone who would want to kill Mr. King?"

"I have no idea ... this is shocking to me and a real nightmare. He was like a father to me —"

"Do you remember your father, Tommy Jordan?" Lindsey asked.

"Yeah, I remember him. What about you, were you one of those people who gave up looking for his killer?" Ayesha asked getting upset at the fact she'd just learned after ten years.

Indeed, Lindsey knew her father, as well as Cranmer. But they weren't a part of investigating him. It was out of their hands and placed into the FBI hands after all the murders, allegedly ordered by Tommy Jordan, got out of control.

"Yes, I know your father. Am I one of those who gave up looking for his killer? No, I'm not, Ayesha. No man or woman deserves to die harshly, no matter what people think of them," Lindsey explained,

"So, why did y'all stop looking?"

"Ayesha, the Philadelphia locals had no jurisdiction to go after your father—"

"I meant his killer," Ayesha retorted sternly.

"And I meant his killers, too ... no one saw nothing and the FBI was in charge —"

"Whatever, you crackers was glad to see my daddy in a body bag!" Ayesha stated, then stepped out of the SUV.

"Ayesha, where are you going?" Lindsey asked as she exited the SUV with Ayesha and caught up with her as she headed for the back door of the funeral home. Lindsey grabbed Ayesha by her shoulder and got an unexpected reaction. Ayesha quickly grabbed Lindsey by her wrist as she spun around and looked Lindsey in her eyes, just seconds away from snapping her wrist.

"Woman, don't you ever put your hands on me. Do you hear me?" Ayesha said sternly, then shoved Lindsey's hand away. Lindsey was shocked at Ayesha's agility and realized that Ayesha was trained in some profession. As both women stared at each other, the back door opened and Cranmer stepped out, surprised to see them. He immediately sensed the tension amongst the two women.

"Is everything okay?" Cranmer asked while looking at his partner, who was staring Ayesha down, stunned at her agility.

"Yeah Cranmer, we was just on our way inside," Lindsey said in spite of Cranmer advising her to stay put. Ayesha turned around and looked at Cranmer.

"Will I be able to see him?" Ayesha asked Cranmer.

"Yeah … but let me warn you, it's not a pretty sight," Cranmer warned Ayesha.

"I'm a big girl, I can handle myself," Ayesha said.

"Come," Cranmer said, then walked back towards the back door. The trio walked inside the funeral home and were met by a Mortician wearing a monocle on his right eye. He was an old white man, on the chubby side, and had a head full of grey hair.

"Okay, Charlie, let's do this," Cranmer said.

"Follow me," Charlie said in a creepy voice, then led the trio down a dimly lit hallway. When they got to a door on the right, Charlie stopped, and inserted a key into the door. Before he allowed everyone in, he warned them.

"It's cold, so brace yourself for winter."

Yeah, he's a damn creep Ayesha thought, as she entered the freezer or still on a gurney. Ayesha saw two bodies on top of a table and gurneys

71

with body bags on them, lined up next to each other. Ayesha couldn't help but think of the fact that every living person was subject to death. She watched as Charlie walked up to a gurney and checked the name tag.

"Caution, we haven't done nothing to Mr. King yet, so he's still in the condition he was brought over from the crime scene," Charlie warned everyone, then proceeded to unzip the body bag. When Ayesha saw Mr. King's bullet riddled face, all the air in her left momentarily.

"Oh, my God," Ayesha exclaimed as tears filled from her eyes in a flood. The sight of Mr. King's bloody face began to transform her every second she stared at him. "Last time I saw my father alive, he had a bloody face as well," Ayesha stated in a voice that she didn't recognize as her own.

"Are you going to be okay, Ayesha?" Cranmer asked, never once thinking of the psychological effect that Mr. King's condition could have on her. Detective Lindsey stood and watched Ayesha closely. She was still stunned from how Ayesha reacted outside.

"I'm fine, thank you for bringing me here, sir," Ayesha said then kissed Mr. King on his cold forehead.

"We will work our ass off trying to find the killer," Cranmer said to Ayesha when she turned around and took a look at all the other gurneys, and the two bodies on the table; who were two black teens.

"What happened to them," Ayesha asked while pointing at the table.

"Gunned down a couple days ago, it's nothing new in this city, right," Charlie informed Ayesha as he zipped Mr. King's body bag back up and walked around the gurney and up to the trio.

"So, we're done here, right?" Charlie asked as he led the trio back out into the hallway.

"Thank you, Charlie, —"

"Cranmer, you're okay pal," Charlie waved Cranmer off. Lindsey's silence bothered Cranmer and it only confirmed that something occurred between her and Ayesha outside his presence.

The entire ride back to Ayesha's condo complex was silent while

Cranmer's country music emanated from the speakers at a low volume. Cranmer dropped Ayesha off back at her car and gave her his card.

"If you need me, don't hesitate to call me, Ayesha," Cranmer told Ayesha.

"I won't … thanks so much," Ayesha said then exited the SUV. Cranmer pulled off the second the door was closed.

"What's the matter, Lindsey?" Cranmer asked as he turned the radio completely off.

"I don't think that was a good ideal."

"I didn't realize it until it was too late," Cranmer retorted.

"So, you saw what I saw also, huh?" Lindsey asked.

"What did you see, Lindsey?"

"The something you saw that prompted your bad ideal," Lindsey retorted.

"He was her psychotherapist that helped her get over the murder of her father … so who will be his replacement is what I'm wondering. She seems bright, and that wasn't no factitious display of grief back there," Lindsey explained.

"I do agree with that, it was the reason I decided to bring her. She wanted closure—"

"And she wanted revenge, Cranmer," Lindsey added, expressing her concern.

"Do you think she knows the killer?" Cranmer asked.

"Cranmer, I don't know what she knows, but I do know that she is an angry bomb waiting to explode. She lost two men that were fathers to her, and has a psychological problem."

"Let's just trust that she'll be okay mentally. I think she feels good that she got closure … we just have to work this one with all we have, Lindsey. We have a long list of other patients to investigate, I say we get started on that as soon as the sun comes up," Cranmer insisted as he pulled into the Philadelphia precinct.

"That sounds like a good start," Lindsey agreed, as Cranmer parked in his assigned parking space.

"What was that about behind the funeral home between you two?" Cranmer asked.

"Her father is a touchy conversation," Lindsey said, then explained to Cranmer what occurred between her and Ayesha. "I was really stunned at how quick she moved Cranmer, she definitely has some type of training."

"Let's not forget that Mr. King was a Master in Martial Arts, and ancient arts as well," Cranmer reminded Lindsey.

"I guess if he was like a father to her that he would teach her a thing or two, huh?" Lindsey replied.

"I would if I was him," Cranmer retorted.

"Yeah," said Lindsey. "Let's get inside. I'll make us some coffee," Lindsey said as she exited the SUV with Cranmer and walked inside the Philadelphia precinct.

Both detectives were exhausted and had been working on Mr. Kings case since leaving the crime scene. Cranmer and Lindsey both operated off the same policy as any other homicide detectives. The next twenty-four hours would be very intense and important to them, because of the forty-eight-hour logic. If no leads popped up in the investigation, Mr. King's case would fall into the statistics of cold cases – unsolved.

From the looks of it thus far we might as well start looking for file tags, because there's no lead in this case, Cranmer thought as he entered the homicide department.

CHAPTER 11

*I*t's been two days since the devastating news of the Master's murder had come to her. Ayesha was all cried out now, and just wanted to make sure the Master's soul rested in peace. He had no next of kin, so she paid for the private funeral that was held at the Yate's Funeral Home, then had him cremated. She kept his ashes in a golden box and would release them into the ocean in Miami, Florida, where he desired his ashes to be released in his will. Ayesha was thankful for Grandma Elsa, who walked her through the funeral arrangements. Without Grandma Elsa, she didn't believe that things would have gone well. She had a shoulder to cry on, just like when she was only nine years old at her father's funeral.

Today, Ayesha woke up with a new attitude and wanted a new look. Pulling up to the "Hair and Beauty Salon" on 76th and Kanner in South Philly, Ayesha doubled checked her decision of showing up.

"There's no turning back girl, go do what you got to do," Ayesha encouraged herself. "Okay …" she said as she grabbed her purse and keys from the ignition. "No turning back," she continued to encourage herself as she stepped out of her .745. Ayesha waited for a car to pass by before she strutted across the street towards the salon. There were a couple hustlers hanging out front sitting on the hood of their cars.

"Damn Ma, who you is?" one of the hustlers asked as he walked up on Ayesha before she could get to the door. He was checking her out in her lustrous mini-skirt, v-shaped blouse and Bebe heels. When Ayesha looked at the hustler, she took in how handsome he was, and decided to put on her good girl attitude.

"You walking up to a stranger, are you sure that's safe?" Ayesha asked the hustler.

He licked his lips and then pulled on his cap that had a green "P" on the front. He was a chocolate complexion, which wasn't her type, but he was handsome and muscular.

"Naw'll, that's not safe. But this is Raekon's block baby, so I'm always checking for passports. Know what I mean?" Raekon replied then licked his lips again. *Damn, I bet he could eat some pussy good the way he licking them lips,* Ayesha thought.

"So, you're the next Tommy Gun, huh?" Ayesha asked.

"Naw'll, I just help take over what he left behind, Ma. Enough of that nigga. What's yo' name?" Raekon asked Ayesha, who'd just bridled herself from grabbing Raekon around his neck. She didn't appreciate the disrespect, and she saw that he was bragging about a takeover." *If these his streets, then he knows something that's been forgotten for ten years now,* Ayesha thought. Instead of exploding, she decided to play it cool.

"My name is Keke ... now, could you please excuse me I have an appointment to get to," Ayesha said, then walked off from Raekon. Before she could open the door, Raekon was there opening it up for her like a gentleman.

"Thanks, Raekon," she said seductively.

"Just fuck with me when you come out ... I'll be waiting for you —"

"I'll think about it," Ayesha said, then walked inside the salon. She could feel Raekon staring at her ass, and knew that she had him. When she turned around, she found him mesmerized. To rub it in, in a sexy way, Ayesha rubbed her ass with her hands and placed her hands on her hips, as she waited at the counter.

Damn! Raekon thought, then closed the door.

"Ayesha! Come over here!" Ayesha's classmate named Katrina shouted throughout the salon. Ayesha walked behind the counter and

AN HOUR LATER, Ayesha pulled up to the Hilton hotel on 123rd and Congress. She wore a black cap over her head and dark sunglasses to carry out her disguise. She called Raekon from a track phone and was directed to room #512. Ayesha walked inside the Hilton hotel and got straight on the elevator. She was lucky to be the only one going up to the fifth floor. When the elevator made it to the fifth floor, she got off and strutted down the hallway, passing a couple and a room service lady before she made it to room #512. She knocked twice before Raekon came to open the door with just a towel on and his thick Cuban link gold chain. *Damn, this nigga got the perfect body!* Ayesha thought as she stared at Raekon pretending to be speechless.

"Are you okay Ma ... I see you brought a packing bag, you must plan on staying all week with me," Raekon said, acknowledging the duffel bag in Ayesha's hand. The Adidas sweat suit Ayesha had on and the hat and shades told Raekon that Ayesha was playing the undercover role.

"Come in baby, and let me take my time with you," Raekon said as he stepped aside to let Ayesha in.

Ayesha stepped inside and allowed Raekon to lock the door. While she looked around the room for any hidden camera's, Raekon came up behind her and put her in his arms. Ayesha could feel his dick erected on her ass.

"So, you had to come low key, I see. That means I ain't the lucky man, huh?" Raekon said as he planted soft kisses on the nape of Ayesha's neck.

"If he was the lucky one ... I wouldn't be here," Ayesha said as she turned around and rubbed Raekon on his massive muscular chest.

Raekon grabbed a hand full of Ayesha's ass in his palms, then started sucking on Ayesha's neck. Ayesha saw that it was a good time to make her move. She quickly delivered an uppercut blow to Raekon's jaw and knocked him unconscious. Before Raekon's body could hit the floor, Ayesha held him up, then dragged him to the bed. The towel on his waist unfastened and fell to the floor, exposing his enormous sized dick. *Damn, this nigga got a monster ... too bad I'll have to pass,* Ayesha thought as she positioned him in the center of the bed.

She then grabbed her duffel bag and pulled out a pair of double hand-cuffs and cuffed Raekon's hands to the bed posts. She then pulled out duct tape and taped his mouth shut. When Raekon came back around, he saw Ayesha sitting on the bed next to him Indian-style.

"Hey there, Raekon ... so tell me, who do I talk to about returning my father's turf back to him?" Ayesha asked Raekon.

"Oh, let me take this off ... "Ayesha said then snatched the duct tape from Raekon's mouth. "Now talk," she retorted.

"Bitch, what the fuck is you talking about?" Raekon asked, Ayesha grabbed her 9mm silencer, cocked it back, then aimed at Raekon, whose eyes expanded in his head.

"I'mma ask you one time to tone it down. Now, who killed Tommy Gun and Quavis back in the day?" Ayesha asked Raekon.

"Tommy Gun is yo' dad?"

"That's not an answer. I don't like repeating myself, either," Ayesha said sternly.

"Listen, I'm not from around here ... I'm from the DC area, Ma. I only heard of Tommy Gun. So, I can't tell you shit I don't know —"

Psst! Psst! Psst!

Ayesha shot Raekon between his eyes before he could say anything else. She then took a crimson lipstick from her duffel bag and applied a thick layer to Raekon's lips.

"There you go, now you have something to lick, baby," Ayesha said, then gathered her things to leave the hotel, like she'd came – in disguise, and leaving the bedroom window open.

CHAPTER 12

"*H*ot 72" turned out to be a knockout track for Young Zoe. People were going crazy over the dis track he responded back to Breezy with. Breezy himself was impressed by the heated lyrics on the track. Young Zoe made sure he wasn't incriminating himself further then what would be circumstantial. Breezy, like the world, was misled to believe that "Hot 72" was all about seventy-two bars of straight spitting harsh remarks about Breezy's weak dis track. Boss was happy to hear from his boy Bruce, who had good news for him. When Boss walked into the P.I.'s office on 120th and Jenkins, he was greeted by Tonya, Bruce's secretary.

"Hello, Mr. Brown ... Mr. Hines is in his office waiting on you. Come right this way, will you," Tonya said, then escorted Boss to Bruce's office.

While walking through the hall, Boss couldn't help but stare at Tonya's nice, firm ass. She was biracial and had a banging body, but unlike a lot of women that Boss ran into, Tonya had a big ass diamond on her wed finger indicating that she was happily married. When Boss and Tonya made it to the office, Tonya opened the door and stuck her head in.

"Mr. Hines, your appointee is here on time, sir."

"Thank you, Tonya bring him on in," Bruce stated then hung up the phone on his desk. Tonya stepped aside and let Boss enter the office, then shut the door behind him.

"What's good, bra?" Boss spoke as he took a seat in the plush chair in front of Bruce's desk.

"Like I told you bra, I would handle business. I have photos of all three Ayesha's. Turns out that one of them is the daughter of legendary Tommy Gun."

"Really?" Boss said, with a raised brow.

"That's what I said," Bruce retorted the handed Boss over a file.

"Inside are three sets of multiple photos of each woman, take a look and tell me if one of them is yours," Bruce said as he grabbed an imported cigar from his desk drawer, and put it in his mouth.

Boss opened up the file and saw that the first set of photos wasn't the Ayesha he was looking for. When he got to the second set, his heart beat accelerated, as he stared at the beautiful woman in the picture. It was the same Ayesha from the club, and it was evident that she was the daughter of Tommy Gun. He knew that there was a familiarity about her from day one. He just would've never expected to ever see the little girl he last saw ten years ago, grow up to be strikingly gorgeous. As Bruce chewed on his cigar, he took notice of how calm Boss was remaining. But he hadn't missed the flinch, and Boss was still on the first set of photos of the second Ayesha.

"I reckon she's their son." Bruce said then lit his cigar with a pistol lighter.

"Yeah … Ayesha T. Jordan, how'd you figure she is Tommy Gun's daughter?" Boss asked as he flipped to the next photo of Ayesha walking out the salon with a new makeover. He recognized one of his Sergeants named Raekon all in her grill putting his mack down. *From the smile on Ayesha's face, Raekon seemed to have scored,* Boss considered.

"I did a little research on them all, just in case you needed it," Bruce replied exhaling thick cloud of smoke.

"I appreciate that," Boss said as he closed the file and stood out of his seat.

"No problem son … Bruce will always be here for you, bra."

"I'mma get up with you later —"

"You know where to find me at, Boss," Bruce said as Boss walked to the door of his office.

"I got cha," Boss retorted then exited Bruce's office

When Boss got outside and hopped into the back seat of the luxury Lincoln Town Car, his driver Tank turned around and dropped a bombshell of news to him.

"Yo' Boss ... Word is around that Raekon's body was found at the big "H" an hour ago."

"Get the fuck out of here!" Boss exclaimed.

"It's serious, son," Tank retorted.

"Get me to the studio, Tank," Boss said as he dialed Young Zoe's number.

"What's good, Fat Boy?" Young Zoe answered.

"Raekon's dead and I got some news for you, stay put," Boss said.

"'Em here, Fat Boy" Young Zoe retorted then hung up the phone.

*　*　*

AYESHA WAS REALLY DIGGING the dis track that Young Zoe had responded to Breezy with. What she loved the most was that Young Zoe attacked Breezy about putting Tommy Gun in his track. Young Zoe shot back proclaiming how much Tommy Gun meant to him and that he would never associate with a guy like Breezy. A big score in Ayesha's book.

"Now that's how a Philly nigga spit," Ayesha said after hearing the dis track on her radio in her kitchen. She was eating a large pizza delivered from Pizza Hut and thinking on her next kill. She realized that no call interrupted her while attending Mr. King's funeral, and was grateful that no call came. Ayesha turned up the radio when she heard the breaking local news.

"Earlier today a room service employee at the Hilton hotel in South Philly found a Raekon Adams murdered. Sorry for this young man's death, people. We have to come to a stop with killing our own people," the radio host stated. "Yeah well, let's start with bringing my daddy back," Ayesha expressed, then took a bite out of her cheese topping pizza. Ayesha house phone began ringing and she wondered whom it was. *Maybe it's Grandma Elsa,* she thought as she stood from the table and walked over to the cordless phone.

"Hello?" Ayesha answered.

"What's up, baby?"

"Who the hell is this?" Ayesha asked perplexed.

"This Tony baby, 'em saying why you be dodging me?" he asked.

"Because I owe you nothing, now get the picture," Ayesha retorted, with transparent spitefulness in her voice.

"Oh, so it's like that, huh?"

"You're the one that's late," said Ayesha,

"Bitch, fuck you," Tony said, finally tired of dealing with the attitude.

"Okay … I will," Ayesha said then hung up the phone.

"I'mma fuck you real good, and teach you 'bout that mouth," Ayesha said then walked back to the table where she sat down and resumed eating her pizza. Ayesha knew where Tony laid his head at and had no problem being his bitch.

"That's where you nigga's get it twisted when you think you could talk to a bitch any king of way!" Ayesha said then smiled impishly. *I got yo' bitch, nigga!* Ayesha thought.

* * *

WHEN BOSS INFORMED Young Zoe about Ayesha T. Jordan, Young Zoe was surprised and found himself stuck between a hard rock. He wanted to meet Ayesha himself, in spite of Boss' advice of it being a bad ideal. Young Zoe and Boss were sitting in the back seat of Young Zoe's Hummer H2 limo where the news had been brought to him. Not only were they surprised about seeing Ayesha, they were trying to fathom why was one of their men found dead in a hotel hours after he'd met with Ayesha.

"Do you think she's connected?'" Boss asked as he held a glass of Remy on rocks in his hand and was smoking on a phat hydro blunt.

"I can't see why … especially if he wasn't robbed, Fat Boy," Young Zoe retorted.

"She lives in a condo, drives a bad ass .745 … do you think she's living off of Tommy Gun's money?" Boss asked.

"Acourse … it'll be insane not to consider it, 'em still on a decision to meet her. I just don't know how to get to her without looking like a stalker."

"I told you son, that's not a good ideal, she better off dead," Boss said.

"We had a chance to do that ten years ago, if it wasn't no threat then, than it ain't no threat now," Young Zoe said then looked at the time on his Rolex.

"I gotta get back inside to record the last two tracks to my mixtape, Fat Boy. I'mma keep these pictures, keep your ears open about Raekon, and trust me, I got this," Young Zoe assured Boss while holding up the file with Ayesha's photos inside.

"When I fuck her brains out, than I might consider killing her. Until then, I want to pay Tommy Gun a favor, man," Young Zoe said, then exited the Hummer H2 limo, leaving Boss alone.

Damnit, I hate when he thinks with the wrong head. I don't trust nothin' about this bitch, Boss thought then made an exit from the Hummer H2 limo, and returned to his Lincoln Town Car.

"Take me to the crib, Tank," Boss said to his driver. As they drove away, Boss pulled out his iPhone and called up one of his goons named Taz, who stood five-feet-eight-inches, 220 pounds of solidness, and was a DC-known killer rolling with Boss.

"Hello?" Taz answered on the second ring.

"Yeah, this Boss … I need you to handle business tonight," Boss said.

"I got you, Boss," Taz said knowing exactly what the big man needed handled. Taz was black as midnight like a lurking black panther.

"I'll be watching," Boss retorted then hung up the phone.

* * *

WHEN THE PROSTITUTE Tina Bell saw the limousine pull up to the curb and stop in front of her, Tina's heart begins to accelerate. She was coming up short on the Boss' money and she had been anticipating the visit. But not so soon.

Damnit I'm in no condition to deal with her bullshit, Tina thought as the back window to the limousine came down, and she saw her Boss' face.

"Get inside, Tina ... I have to talk to you," Bianca ordered Tina. Tina's hesitation caused Bianca to get upset, and whenever Bianca was upset, it was best to steer away from her until she calmed down.

"Bitch, I said get in the car!" Bianca raised her voice the same time one her bodyguards stepped out the limo from the passenger seat and grabbed Tina Bell by her arm. Tina immediately snatched her arm away from the brawny bodyguard.

"I can help myself, I don't need your help!" Tina Bell shouted, then opened the back door and climbed inside.

Once inside, Tina Bell became more nervous, something that always occurred when she was in the presence of Bianca. To her, Bianca was an untouchable Pimptress who could have a woman killed with just one word. Despite prostitution being her only source of income Tina Bell was an afraid seventeen-year-old single mom who had a cinnamon complexion and stood 5'5" 125 pounds

"Tina Bell ... next time you make me raise my voice I will have your voice box. Do we understand each other?" Bianca asked Tina Bell in a calm voice while holding a glass of champagne in her hands. Tina Bell looked Bianca in her eyes and took in the expensive fur coat she had on. She couldn't help but think of how unfair it was for Bianca to take 75% of the money she made prostituting. Before she got Bianca mad again, Tina Bell answered Bianca.

"Yes Bianca ... I understand you."

"Good, now, Bianca need to know something ... you prostitute every night, all day long seven days out the week. Why the fuck are my numbers not adding up when it comes to you, Tina Bell?"

For a moment, Tina Bell contemplated what she would tell Bianca before she spoke.

"Business hasn't been good for me, Bianca, especially when you have Rosa on the same block as me. All the customers go to her, and I'm left standing out in the rain," Tina Bell explained.

"So, do I need to relocate you?" Bianca asked.

"That'll be great if you could, Bianca," Tina Bell retorted while scratching the inside of her arms. Bianca saw the signs of a friend and grabbed Tina Bell by her inner forearm. Bianca immediately saw the needle tracks and became upset.

"Bitch, you're shooting up dope!" Bianca shouted, then slapped Tina Bell in her face vigorously, spilling most of her drink

"No!" Tim lied as she shielded herself from Bianca's attack. Bianca placed her almost empty drink in the limousine's console, then began to remove her jewelry from her neck.

"Bitch, you gonna sit her and lie to me?"

While Bianca removed her jewelry, Tina Bell cried and tried to exit the limo, but the door was being blocked by Bianca's bodyguard.

"Please, Bianca, you don't understand —"

"Understanding that my hoes will be drug free is all that concerns me, bitch!" Bianca shouted as she yanked Tina Bell by her weave and began to punch her in her face until she had the strength to pull away and ball up into a corner.

"Tina Bell ..." Bianca said breathlessly, "I took you in and gave you a place to lay your head if you promised me that you would stay off the drugs ... why are you shooting up?"

When Tina Bell looked up, Bianca saw the damage she'd done to Tina Bell's face. She had a closed right eye and blood trickling from her split lip. Bianca didn't feel sorry for what she'd done, she only felt more powerful and in control. Beating her prostitutes had become a habit for Bianca, and had been keeping her prostitutes in check. She wanted them to have the fear of God in them when she came for her money or to gather information like she'd intended to do to Tina Bell.

"Em sorry, Bianca ... I promise you that I will clean up," Tina Bell cried.

"Bitch, you have two weeks to get yourself together or I will run yo' ass out of my city, and anywhere I catch you after I tell you to leave ... I will kill you," Bianca said sternly.

"Okay, Bianca ..." Tina Bell said, then wiped her bloody mouth with a napkin she pulled from her purse.

"Now tell me ... what detective came snooping around the other day, and what did she have to say?" Bianca asked.

"It was the black lady Camilla and her partner the white man name Eastwood or something like that," Tina Bell said as she dabbed at the trickling blood from her lip.

"They were looking for someone to inform them of who was last seen with Ciara," Tina Bell informed Bianca of the prostitute named Ciara who everyone knew that Bianca had killed a couple weeks ago. The police had found Ciara's body inside a dumpster behind a warehouse after getting a call from the owner of the warehouse.

"And what did you tell them?" Bianca asked.

"I told them that I never knew who Ciara was or ever seen her around," Tina Bell informed Bianca who took it as the truth.

"Keep it like that, Tina Bell, or else you'll join your friend Ciara. Are we understood?"

"Yes, Bianca, we are understood," Tina Bell retorted.

"Good, now please get out my face bitch, and get yo' shit together ... Al! let her out," Bianca screamed to her bodyguard, who was once her mother's bodyguard during her Pimptress reign.

Al opened the back door and Tina Bell quickly exited the limousine and hurried down the street with her head down. As the limousine pulled away from the curb, Bianca called up her new boyfriend that she'd made official two weeks ago. Boyfriends didn't come often for Bianca. Some men just couldn't accept her profession, and deal with the fact that for the right price, a handsome man would be able to rent her for the night. She liked her boyfriend a lot and loved how he respected her hustle. She knew that he had women going nuts over him, and that on some occasions, he chose to fuck some of them. She didn't care, it was all game if he was hers at the end of the night. On the third ring, her boyfriend's voice spilled into her ears.

"What's up, baby?" Breezy asked.

"Where are you?"

"'Em at the studio, about to wrap up this track. What's up?" Breezy asked.

"I'm on my way over ... it's getting' late and I need some company tonight," Bianca said in a sexy voice that turned Breezy on.

"'Em down with that ... come through baby," Breezy said then hung up the phone.

Bianca smiled as she refilled her glass with champagne. She was glad to hear that the detectives were lost at finding leads to Ciara's murder. Now she was just ready to celebrate in the arms of Breezy, who she saw as Philadelphia's next hottest rapper. Though she agreed like everyone else that Young Zoe's "Hot 72" was a hot come back, her North Philly boyfriend was still the best in her eyes.

She had the money to endow in Breezy's rap career and she would, already having her mind made up. She wanted to see him blow up and be in the light with him. Breezy wasn't naïve to the dangers in the streets, even in his own back yard he stayed strapped and ready for war. With the dis track he'd put out and the infamous gorgeous Pimptress on his team, Breezy knew that he was subject to automatic beef. Breezy didn't give a fuck about how Young Zoe fans would take the track He was his own man, and was known for putting in work for North Philly before he started rapping about it. Breezy stood tall at five-foot-nine, 175 pounds solid, and fooled many as being a pretty boy who still was rocking braids. He had plans to shack up with a bad bitch named Zo'Mami from North Philly until his #1 called him and caused him to abort. Breezy was nose wide open about Bianca and respected her grind 100%.

That bitch be tryna suck the brown off a nigga dick, Breezy thought as he sat back in the La-Z-Boy and waited for Bianca to hit him up informing him that she was outside. His homeboy Trouble was sitting at his computer putting his final touch on Breezy's hit he'd just completed. All Breezy could think about was Bianca. She was definitely a game changer, because Breezy had never turned Zo'Mami down, who was a bad bitch herself. Breezy saw his iPhone lighting up and saw that it was Bianca hitting him up.

There she go, Breezy thought flattered.

"What's up, beautiful?"

"'Em outside daddi" Bianca retorted in a sexy voice.

"'Em coming," Breezy said then hung up the phone.

"Trouble, a nigga on go mode, I'mma hit you up in the a.m." Breezy informed Trouble as he jumped up out the La-Z-Boy and threw his hoodie over his head.

"Alright my nigga, I'mma finish the Master touch on this hit and get me some rest," Trouble said while rubbing his eyes.

"You do that son, and rest well. We got a show tomorrow," Breezy said as he walked towards the front door.

"Stay up, son."

"Always son," Breezy retorted.

When Breezy stepped outside, he was expecting to see Bianca in her Pearl S-Class Benz, but instead saw an awaiting black limousine with the back door open, and Bianca's bodyguard Al standing outside the back door. *Now this is a boss bitch,* Breezy thought as he climbed into the back seat and put Bianca in his arms. The sexy attire she had on Breezy quickly learned that she was pantiless.

"Damn Ma, if I'd known you were pulling up like the president than I would have brought the champagne —"

Before Breezy could finish Bianca quieted him with a sloppy kiss. Breezy slid his hands inside her mink coat and caressed her delicate curves, as he laid Bianca back on the back seat. Breezy began planting kisses on Bianca's neck and slowly immersed while sliding up Bianca's mini dress. Bianca was melting at Breezy's every touch and wanted him to take her to a sexual paradise, as they cruised through the city limits.

"Mmm," Bianca moaned when she felt Breezy's tongue swipe across her clitoris.

"Baby?!" Bianca panted, as Breezy removed his gun from his waist and laid it on the floor, then unfastened his belt.

"Baby, do you have a condom?" Bianca purred.

"Damn!" Breezy exclaimed, then sat back in his seat and stared at his erect dick. Bianca sat up with a smile on her face and grabbed

Breezy's dick. Slowly, she stroked him and licked the pre-com from the tip of his dick.

"Al, stop at the first "Wawa" please!" Bianca screamed to Al behind the blind board.

"I got you, B!" Al retorted.

"Keep a spare, you never know when I might want what's mines," Bianca said to Breezy the resumed sucking his dick.

"I got you baby," Breezy retorted as he watched Bianca suck his dick with perfection.

Damn, this bitch is blowing my mind! Breezy thought as he rubbed his hands on Bianca's soft ass cheeks. He slid two fingers inside her wet pussy, and finger stroked her slow.

"Mmm!"

"Shit!" Breezy exclaimed as he exploded inside Bianca's mouth. Bianca swallowed Breezy's load, then sucked his dick until he was all clean again. When the limo stopped Breezy and Bianca saw that they were at a "Wawa" gas station.

"Hurry, so we can get home," Bianca said as she fixed her hairdo.

"Anything to drink?"

"I just drunk what I needed, now go," Bianca said.

Breezy stepped out of the limo and felt good as the cool air hit him in his face. As he walked towards the front door of the station, he felt naked for some odd reason. He felt for his gun and realized that he was armless.

Shit, pussy got a nigga slipping bad! Breezy thought as he continued on into the store. Once inside, Breezy pulled out a wad of cash from his jeans and peeled off $2.

"Let me get the gold box on them Mags," Breezy pointed out the condoms behind the counter to the store clerk, then slid her the $2.

"$1.99 sir," the store clerk said as she came back with the box of condoms.

"Bianca!" Breezy shouted, then felt a storm of bullets riddle his body. As Breezy hit the pavement, Al came out with a mac-10 and returned fire, but Taz and his getaway driver were out of the line of fire. Bianca couldn't believe what she'd just saw, and was too shocked to utter a scream like she badly wanted to. When Al opened the back door, Bianca saw Breezy laid out on the bloody pavement with a motionless stare in his eyes.

"B … he's gone, there's no life in him—"

"Noooo!" Bianca shrilled, cutting Al off. She climbed out the back seat and put Breezy's head in her lap as she hugged him. She'd seen death her whole life, but it was the first life taken from her that she actually cared for.

"Breezy!" Bianca cried.

CHAPTER 13

"*P*hiladelphia rapper killed within seventy-two hours of his released dis song towards Young Zoe, the face of Philadelphia. Authorities are now trying to see if the rapper Young Zoe is connected in any way. Anyone with information, please call the Philadelphia tips line at 1-800-P-Tips. I am Yolanda Garner reporting live with your breaking news on Channel 7."

Damn, he really had Breezy knocked off ... that shit is obvious and he don't even care, Ayesha thought as she watched the breaking news of Breezy's death. It was everywhere reporting, the TV, and the radio were no escape from the intense social media. Some earlier news claimed that he was with his girlfriend at the time of his death, and his girlfriend turned out to be the infamous Pimptress. *Who's to say one of her clients didn't do it?* Ayesha thought as she slid into a pair of jeans.

"Well Breezy, you shouldn't have come at a man who you know could have you bodied. Shit, I even wanted to pay you a visit for putting my dad name in your shit. My daddy ain't never fuck with you North Philly nigga's, he ran y'all," Ayesha said amongst herself while getting dressed.

Today was the beginning of her hunt for her father's killer and she was more eager than she'd ever been when going on a mission. She was also preparing herself to go see Governor Jimmy McCarthy of Florida and of the Democrat Party campaign in downtown South Philly. It was her chance to finally see McCarthy in person, and if she was going to vote for him, she wanted to see him in person.

When Ayesha finished dressing herself she sprayed herself with some of her Rihanna perfume, Crush, then proceeded out the front door. When she stepped outside, Ayesha froze in her tracks.

"What the fuck?" she exclaimed, surprised to see a box on her front step.

Inside, she could see a dozen red roses, a white teddy bear, and a box of chocolate candy. *What creep wants to be all sweet today?* Ayesha thought as she bent down and picked up the box. She carried he box to her car and sat it on the passenger seat. When she looked at the box of candy she noticed that it was her favorite chocolate bears she loved as a kid. The only person who'd ever bought her the chocolate bears was her father. The memory almost brought tears to her eyes, but the Murderlicious inside of her was done crying. Her daddy wanted her to be a big girl, and that's exactly what she would do for him. Ayesha picked up the roses and read the note that was attached to the ribbon.

"I just knew from the first time I saw you that you would be someone special. Woman, you've grown into a beautiful lady, and I want you to know that a woman like you deserves the world. Your father gave me a chance, and made me the man I am today. He told me to always strive because when you stop, the world keeps going, as well as your opportunities ... I see a perfect opportunity to make the man we both looked up to proud. It only takes for you to say yes ... call me (717) 605-4327 – "Young Zoe."

"Oh, my God!" Ayesha exclaimed, not believing that she was actually reading a note from Young Zoe.

"He remembers me when I was a little girl, but I don't remember him," Ayesha retorted.

Acourse I don't remember him, Tommy Gun never let anyone come around me but Quavis, she thought remembering how strict her father was about her safety.

"How the hell did he know where I lived at?" Ayesha thought as she started her car with a smile on her face. She couldn't hide how much she was blushing if she wanted to.

"I gotta tell Tamara and Alexis this shit," Ayesha said then pulled out her condo complex with Young Zoe on her mind.

* * *

BIANCA WAS COMPLETELY DEVASTATED and felt like her world was completely taken away from her. She only had her mother Ariel's shoulder to cry on, and was grateful for her mother's support.

"Momma, I know Young Zoe sent the hit, he's a creep and that fat dirty bitch ass nigga Boss not too far from being involved," Bianca expressed theoretically. While laying her head on her mother's lap. They'd been sitting on the sofa for hours after Bianca was released from being questioned. The blood from Breezy's body was still on her thighs dried up, and she was still wearing the blood stained mini dress. Despite the dress being a dark purple the blood stains were visible.

"Baby we know how these streets are, these niggas will kill the nigga who taught them everything. At the end of the day, we don't know who did it so we can't go out there speculating. I feel your pain, Bianca, and I know what it's like to lose a lover. But most importantly I had to grieve today, and hustle tomorrow like shit ain't happen. Stressing about something you can't change will harm you, and break you down, Bianca," Ariel explained to Bianca while rubbing her back.

Bianca raised up and wiped the tears from her face.

"Mom, I wouldn't be able to do this without you … thank you so much for being here for me," Bianca said to her mother as she hugged her.

"You'll be alright baby, now go and get yourself cleaned up, you got some hoes to go collect that check from," Ariel said causing Bianca to laugh, and cheer up a little.

"Mom, you're so full of it!" Bianca said then stormed off to the bathroom to clean the death of Breezy off of her. While in the shower, Bianca cried once more for Breezy, and realized that her mother was right. She couldn't let grief destroy her. *But I could destroy Young Zoe,* Bianca thought.

* * *

AFTER HEARING an empowered speech given by McCarthy, Ayesha knew beyond a doubt that she would give him her vote. Ayesha left the rally an hour ago and had been sitting inside her car watching her friend Tony's front door apartment. He had a guest inside and she didn't want to disturb him. Ayesha contemplated on calling Young Zoe, but she didn't want to put herself in the area that would soon become a highlight, and take the attention from Breezy's murder. She was tired of hearing condolences from his fans, and the radio host talk about the murder. So, she downloaded some of Young Zoe's hits from her iPhone and played them through her Bluetooth device, while she ate her McDonald's, she'd brought along. Ayesha couldn't help but think what a night with Young Zoe would be like. *He's everything that I desire in a man, handsome, brown-skinned, and intelligent,* Ayesha thought, as she sucked soda from her straw. She was listening to Young Zoe's "Hit 72" track that was being liked all around the country, and a hit that was about to take his rap career to an unexpected level of lavish. As much as she tried to remember him, Ayesha just couldn't recall ever being in his presence.

But it felt like we've seen each other before, even at the club. *The way he looked at me was mind-boggling,* Ayesha thought as she shoved a hand full of French fries in her mouth. Ayesha didn't care what people were saying about Young Zoe being responsible for Breezy's death. She just had to worry about if she got involved with him, watching her back for his enemies, too. *I already have too much going on for myself, but if I do fuck with him maybe he could enlighten me on who he thinks killed my father, if not his homie, Boss,* Ayesha thought. She was under the same impression as everyone else. A couple DC niggas took over after his death. It was told by her exes that all the DC niggas were affiliated with Tommy Gun. Ayesha knew that Young Zoe and Boss were close, and it made no sense to her that Boss would be behind her father's murder if Young Zoe was his homie. It just didn't add up to Ayesha when she thought about the possibility.

"Show time," Ayesha said when she looked towards Tony's apartment and saw him standing at the door, bare chested, with a towel wrapped around his waist, as he watched his booty call chick leave in her bad conditioned Honda.

"I can't believe I ever gave this dirty foot ass nigga any play," Ayesha waited until the girl was gone and Tony had closed the door before she started her car and pulled into the parking space the Honda had just left. Ayesha grabbed her leather gloves from off the passenger's seat where her lunch was, and slid them on her hands. She then pulled a skully over her head to cover her ears. She hated the cold and her ears were her downfall against the cold and men who discovered her G-spot. Ayesha stepped out of the car and walked up to Tony's door. She knocked on the door three times then waited for him to open up. When Tony opened the door and saw Ayesha, he was surprised.

"Damn, so you've changed your mind, huh?" Tony asked Ayesha while holding on to his towel.

"I don't take what you say to heart …plus, I admit I've been kinda notty lately! Can I come in?" Ayesha asked seductively, with her hands in her coat pocket. *Two bitches in the same hour … damn Tony, you bad!* Tony prided himself.

"Come in baby, and let me show you how much I forgive you," Tony said then stepped aside for Ayesha to come inside the apartment. Ayesha stepped inside the apartment and waited for Tony to lock the door. When Tony turned around, Ayesha spun quickly and drop kicked Tony. As Tony slid down the door Ayesha saw that his eyes were rolled behind his head. *TKO bitch ass nigga!*

"I told you that I had yo' bitch, nigga," Ayesha said as she dragged Tony to the living room. While applying lipstick to Tony's lips, he was coming back to consciousness. Tony blinked his eyes twice to subside the blurry vision he had. He could only see her figure for a moment until he saw Ayesha clearly aiming a gun at him.

"Ayesha, no!"

Psst! Psst! Psst! Psst! ... as Tony tried coming at Ayesha she pulled the trigger until the clip was empty.

Satisfied with her art, Ayesha left the apartment unnoticed to any of the neighbors. While sitting in traffic at an intersection Ayesha's Verizon track phone received an incoming call with a smile on her face Ayesha answered the phone.

"Hello?"

"Please enter your code name please." –*Beep!* Murderlicious, Ayesha quickly typed in then waited for her representative to come on the line.

* * *

YOUNG ZOE persistently continued to check his iPhone every thirty minutes waiting on Ayesha to call him. All day he'd been approached by detectives trying to link him to Breezy's death but he knew the protocol. – "Never talk to the police alone."

Every moment he thought about Ayesha he couldn't believe that the little girl he'd seen ten years ago had grown up to be a gorgeous woman. *She's definitely wifey material,* Young Zoe thought while sitting on his plush sofa inside his condo in Pittsburgh. No one knew of his condo in Pittsburgh, not even Boss. It was a place where he could run off the face of the earth, away from his fans and entourage and just be himself. Being that he had time to look at everything that's been going on, Young Zoe thought about the Pimptress Bianca. It was new to him that she was dating Breezy. *Had I known she was dating the chump, I probably would have spared him on Ariel's face,* Young Zoe thought then took a pull off of his blunt.

"The bitch should be thinking me that she who she is today, and be glad that I didn't know shit about running a prostitution ring or else Ariel would've been a dead soul," Young Zoe said amongst himself going back to when him and Boss took Tommy Gun and Quavis out the game.

"It's never too late for anything," Young Zoe repeated the words Tommy Gun used to tell him. Young Zoe didn't like the fact that

Bianca was even chilling with the North Philly cats, and regulating the prostitution on his turf. What Young Zoe didn't know, due to being too focused on his career, was that the Pimptress Bianca had grown into a powerful woman – more powerful than her mother had ever been. Young Zoe iPhone chime emanating his "Hot 72" track as a ringtone. When he looked at the caller ID and saw that it wasn't the unfamiliar number that he was looking for, Young Zoe pressed the side button and sent the caller to his voice mail.

"I guess she gone play hard ball with the champ," Young Zoe said then took a pull on his blunt.

* * *

IT WAS 9:00 P.M. when Detective Cranmer and Lindsey pulled up to the crime scene in South Philly, Village Park Apartments. They were called because a second victim had popped up with lipstick on their lips, and they were both males. Together the duo crossed over the yellow tape and entered the apartment where they found Tony McQueen, a small-time hustler, laying on the floor naked with innumerable gun holes in his torso area. And a crimson brand of lipstick on his lips. The two previous detectives who'd been assigned to the case came walking out the back room. Crime scene investigators were all over the place trying to find evidence that they would never find of the killer.

"Good to see you two," Detective Camilla McAdams said to Cranmer and Lindsey. She was a tough detective, and the first black detective in the jurisdiction of South Philly. Though she wasn't attractive, she'd once been called the hand-me-down girl after dating multiple men on the force. It was her weakness, but her strength was nailing the bad guys. Behind her was her partner Eastwood, who was a specialist in firearms, and was called the Young Brad Pitt.

"It's good to see you too, Camilla. So, what mess do we have ourselves?" Detective Lindsey asked, while looking around at all the activity.

"Found him an hour ago by a family member —"

"In what relation?" Cranmer asked while putting on gloves.

"Sister. No one seen who was last seen with him—"

"And let me guess, no one heard any shots either?" Lindsey asked Camilla.

"Exactly, you know the Philly protocol" Camilla retorted.

What you think Eastwood?" Cranmer asked Eastwood who eyes were on Tony's body.

"Close range shots definitely, small-time hustler ..." Eastwood said scratching his bald head.

"The lipstick in both cases throws me off. We've taken samples of the lipstick. We just have to wait and see what comes back, Cranmer ... but from the looks of it, we have a match already\," Eastwood explained. Cranmer nodded his head at Eastwood then walked over to Tony. He knelt down and took a look at the lipstick on Tony's lip. *What the fuck is going on here?* Cranmer thought, hoping that some clue would jump out to him.

"What's the caliber?" Detective Lindsey asked while standing over Cranmer's shoulder. Cranmer picked up up a shell casing and looked at the stamped caliber on the back of the shell.

".9mm"

"Same caliber used in Raekons murder," Lindsey said,

"Yep ..." Cranmer retorted as he stood up. "Which means we're looking for the same killer," Cranmer retorted,

"That's great," said Lindsey,

"Good luck," Eastwood retorted, then walked out of the apartment.

"You guys will be okay. If you need me, just call me," Camilla said to Cranmer and Lindsey.

"Thank you, Camilla," Lindsey said as she hugged Camilla then watched her leave the crime scene with her partner.

"I don't like these types of crimes—"

"Why?" Lindsey asked Cranmer.

"Because they make no sense but go real deep ... it's personal. And the first thing we need to be doing is finding out who is his girlfriend," Cranmer suggested.

"Good luck with that one."

"Why do you say that?" Cranmer asked Lindsey.

"Because he's a small-time hustler, all the girls are his," Lindsey retorted,

"Well, all of them are suspects as well," Cranmer said then looked around at the diligent (CSI) workers dusting everything in the apartment.

"Do you think whoever killed Raekon killed Tony, Cranmer?"

"It's possible ... we know that the killer is a woman who disguised her identity well at the hotel ... we just can't put her here, that's the pain in my ass," said Cranmer.

CHAPTER 14

*B*en Scott and his guest, Arnold Bush, exited the 5-star restaurant in Pittsburgh together, surrounded by Ben Scott's bodyguards. When both of them entered the back seat of Ben Scotts limousine, it was as if they sighed together. From the rally to the restaurant was very intense for the both of them, who were expecting danger to erupt at any moment. It was clear to everyone in the world that those who'd contributed to Ben Scott's campaign lately had been assassinated. Despite many folks advising Ben Scott to drop out of the race for the White House and let another Republican pursue. He remained adamant of taking heed, and didn't care that his life was in danger. Arnold Bush, who was the Vice President nominee running against Democrat Vice President nominee Paul Lane, had even suggested for Ben Scott to drop out of the race as well

"Tonight went well, Arnold, we're going to nail these Democrats to the cross like their Catholic Jesus," Ben Scott said while loosening up his tie.

"Yeah it did, and I'd still feel better if I wasn't always looking for a bullet to hit me in my skull —"

"Oh, stop it pal, you're wrecking your own balls for nothing," Ben Scott retorted as he poured Arnold a glass of whiskey.

"Here, have a drink, then promise me that you'll get a good night's sleep?" Ben Scott said then downed his glass of whiskey and immediately poured himself another glass.

"Take it easy pal, I don't want to have to carry you up to your suite," Arnold said to Ben Scott who tried his best to hide his drinking problem from the world. He knew that his problem was safe with Arnold. Had it been anyone else, Ben wouldn't risk a chance for a leak.

"It's the only way that I can stay sane through this entire race."

"Don't worry Ben ..." Arnold said as he gave Ben Scott's shoulder a squeeze. "We're going to win, and when we do, we're going to change this world back to the old world. Hitler failed, but we will prevail, just watch and see," Arnold said to Ben Scott then took a sip from his glass. Ben Scott looked out his window and saw the passing streets, businesses, and luxury homes.

Soon the world would be mine ... six more months if I can stay alive to win it, Ben Scott thought, solemnly.

"What makes you think we'll do better than Hitler did?" Ben Scott asked Arnold while still looking out his window.

"The things we have today in the world, Ben, Hitler dreamed he had in his days," Arnold advised Ben Scott. Ben Scott turned his head and looked at Arnold Bush with an approving smile on his face.

"That's why I like you Arnold, together we will change this world pal, and we will finish what Hitler started," Ben Scott informed Arnold as the limousine pulled up to their hotel.

"Well, let's get some rest. I'll see you in the morning, Mr. President," Arnold said to Ben, then stepped out of the limousine, immediately being swarmed by security. Ben Scott adjusted his tie, preparing to step out the limousine next, until he heard the district sound of gunfire erupt. Not knowing where the shots were coming from, Ben Scott got down on the floor of the limousine and covered his head. *Lord, this is not happening!* Ben Scott thought, timorously.

"Up there on top of the roof!" one of the security guards screamed while pointing at the roof top of a Wawa gas station 200 yards away. The security guards were able to spot the shooter after seeing the fire from the muzzle of the rifle every time the shooter squeezed the trigger. With their weapons aimed at the rooftop and exchanging fire, the security guards ran towards the Wawa gas station.

"Governor Arnold Bush is down ... he's dead!" Ben Scott heard a security guard shrill.

"Damnit! Why tonight fucker!" Ben Scott shouted as more shots erupted.

As the security guards ran towards the Wawa gas station. Ayesha took them down one by one exploding their heads with the M25 sniper rifle.

"Come on bitches," Ayesha said as she continued to hit all moving targets.

The limousine had pulled up precisely at 11:30 P.M., like her representative had informed her. She had no clue whom it was she'd just assassinated. Ayesha was only following her instructions to nail the first man that stepped out of the limo. Then take down a couple security guards. Seeing that her job was done, Ayesha broke down her weapon and placed it back inside the M25 case. When she looked back towards the chilling scenery, she'd created she saw more guards running towards the gas station. With speed, Ayesha ran towards the back of the gas station and climbed down the rope she'd attached to the building. When she hit the ground, she made a dash for the stolen Dodge van she pulled up in. Ayesha hopped in the van and ignited the hot wire successfully. Not wanting to bring attention to herself, she pulled off slowly. When Ayesha turned the corner, three security guards came running up to the van with their guns aimed at her.

Company! Ayesha thought.

"Don't move!" one of the brawny security guards told Ayesha.

"No, it's a mistake, the shooter ran that way, I saw him!" Ayesha exclaimed while pointing West of her location. The security guards were all perplexed seeing that Ayesha was a woman.

"Are you sure, woman!"

"Yes I am. Hurry, go get him!" Ayesha retorted hysterically.

With no further hesitation, the security guards took off running in the direction that Ayesha had led them. Ayesha pulled off simultaneously with no further problems and vanished off into the night.

* * *

IT WAS 2:30 A.M. in the wee hours when Ayesha pulled up to the suburban home in East Philadelphia. She'd ditched the stolen van and splacked an Altima. As soon as she got into the city limits of Philadelphia, she was at the correct address. Seeing the unmarked detective car only confirmed any doubt that existed. Ayesha pulled in behind the unmarked and killed the engine and lights to the Altima. She then stepped out of the car, and walked up to the front door.

"Here it goes," Ayesha exclaimed then rung the doorbell. Ayesha listened to the Christmas tunes emanate throughout the home. Moments later, she heard the door being unlocked. When the door opened, Ayesha saw the detective she'd come to see. He was holding a book in his hands with a pair of reading glasses hanging on the bridge of his nose.

"May I help you, ma'am?" he asked with a raised brow.

"Yeah um —" before Ayesha could finish sucka punched the detective in his chin and knocked him out cold.

When the detective hit the ground, Ayesha removed his weapon from his shoulder holster and released the clip. She then stepped inside and secured her target with his own handcuffs before she did a thoroughly search of the house.

..

* * *

POSITANO, Italy

"SHE'S INCREDIBLE," CIA agent Bill Duncan said to his boss, and Commander of Special Ops "Blue Jay 157". His name was David Landi, an old man of the age sixty-four years old, and had seen a lot of skilled assassins in his time. But none like Murderlicious, who was proving to be the best he'd ever seen at such a young age.

Bill Duncan was his secretary, and the only man he trusted in the business he ran for higher officials than himself in the government. And was responsible for more than a dozen trained assassins across the world. Each assassin had the ultimate choice when they chose to retire, and that was to live by leaving the country they'd lived in, or die as a result in staying. It was a code that every assassin had to live by called the "Code of Silence." A code that Bernard King had broken, when requesting Murderlicious to take his place as he retired. David Landi and his secretary sat in his office staring at the headlines appearing on the TV screen, and both agreed that they had a real monster on their hands.

"I think the Democrats are getting out of hand with this last one Bill," David said to his protégé, then took a sip from his steaming coffee mug.

"Yeah, but name a time when they ever took caution into consideration?"

"Your right … so tell me if I put her and the Terminator together, do you think that they'll succeed in Special Ops Sandy?" David asked his protégé.

Bill Duncan stood up from the plush sofa in front of David's desk and walked towards the black board that David had in his office. Bill Duncan stood at six-foot-two, 220 pounds and was an ex-Marine major at fifty-seven years old. His intelligence and the way he masterminded the government plays, and handled cross seas threats is what landed him a job with the CIA – eventually led him to the Master at erasing the threats to either party of the government. For years, the Democrats had been winning the white house, because of people like David Landi, who wanted the world to be the land of the honey and not a big in debuted, and irresponsible country that the Republicans were promising if they won the election. Bill Duncan grabbed a piece of chalk from the black board and drew two lines on the board.

"Murderlicious and Terminator, two one-of-a-kind killing machines, with about eighteen years of age difference and a complete different mindset ... but they do what it takes to get the job done," Bill Duncan said, then wrote a cryptic code underneath Murderlicious' name.

"This is why we must put them together," Bill Duncan stated, then laid the chalk down, simultaneously dusting his hands off so that no chalk would get on his expensive black suit. David had an approving smile on his face and agreed with his protégé. But as the Commander-in-Chief to the ultimate decision, he felt that Murderlicious needed a little more time in the field before he decided to assign her to a mission like "Special Ops Sandy."

"It's a wonderful ideal Bill, but I must give her more time to develop ... at least until she's twenty-one," David Landi said,

Bill Duncan crossed his legs while sitting on the sofa and wasn't the least surprised to see his partner delay an important mission that, if succeeded, would make them billionaires.

"One more thing, David," Bill Duncan said while holding up his index finger.

"She's doing a good job with her selected victims, just to throw any chance of suspicion that we might be involved in these assassins. I think she should leave her mark on the next missions to get rid of the FBI snooping."

David Landi thought about what his protégé was explaining to him. Murderlicious was leaving all her recent unassigned victims branded with crimson lipstick and nobody knew why she was doing it. *But it was impressive and a state of art itself,* David Landi thought.

"That'll be a good ideal pal ... make sure to inform her at her next assignment," David replied to his protégé, who knew that he would concede in concordance with his recommendation.

"I just hope that the Democrats have their shit together, because the heat is about to come down hard on them, David—"

"That's not our problem. Our job is to get rid of the problem, meaning if they, themselves, become a problem, then we get rid of them too," David Landi expressed.

* * *

WHEN FBI AGENTS Steven Spencer and Jackie Flynn arrived at the massacre scene at the Lebell Hotel in Pittsburgh, they had to force themselves through the enormous crowd of news reporters and nosey attendants of the hotel, along with pedestrians. It took them every bit of fifteen minutes to reach the yellow crime scene tape that was roping off the entrance of the hotel. When both agents ducked underneath the crime scene tape, they immediately met up with their boss, Director Nick Young, who was an experienced veteran to solving serial killer crimes at just forty-five years old.

"Special Agents Spencer and Flynn, it's about time you two arrived," Director Nick Young said to the two best agents he could rely on to assign the massacre case to

"We landed an hour ago, plus fifteen minutes, trying to get through all this media," Agent Flynn retorted, who was the better spokesperson amongst her and Agent Spencer. She was a gorgeous thirty-five-year-old blonde haired woman with adorable blue eyes and resembled the actor Scarlett Johansson.

"Well let's get started, I have a news conference going live in an hour," Young said as he checked the time to his expensive gold Rolex.

Being a black man in his position at such a young age proved that he, himself, could run for President if he wanted to. But seeing what was going on around the world with falling Republican supporters, he wouldn't know whose side to be safe on.

"Sir, are we staying local for this one?" Agent Spencer asked, who resembled Jimmy Kimmel in every aspect, and who was another sharp pencil in the box with an incredible intelligence on saving high crime cases such as assassinations

"I'm afraid that I forgot to tell you to bring along a sleeping bag, sorry about that Spencer," Young said as he turned Spencer around by his shoulders and pointed towards the roof top of the Wawa gas station where (CSI) was gathering evidence.

"On top of that roof, the shooter waited, and shot a round of more than fifty fatal shots ... the first shot taking Governor Arnold Bush in the back of his head. Then the shooter turned his weapon from left to right, like trained in the military ..." Young said demonstrating the actions of the shooting theoretically.

"So, who are we looking for, Flynn?" Young asked Agent Flynn, who was seeing the shooting take place in her mind while staring at all the dead security guards on the ground underneath white shrouds. Blood and entrails were everywhere in the chilling scenery.

"We're definitely looking for a marksman," she retorted then looked at her boss, who released an approving smile.

"One that's targeting Republicans, which makes me ask this question, sir ... who do we have investigating Mr. Jimmy McCarthy and his supporters?" Spencer asked. Director Young put his hands in his pockets and looked at Spencer in his eyes before he spoke.

"Spencer, we don't know if the FBI itself needs to be investigated. I wouldn't undermine my job for nothing and advise you to do the same. I trust you two to work diligently on this case ... and only this case. In a couple days, we will decide where we are going with the links," Director Young said, "Do we understand?" he asked Spencer, who hated Young who carried around a hubris attitude, and thought that he was the black Superman. To keep things at level and to continue to have a job, Spencer said the most prudent response.

"Yes sir ... we got you."

"Good, I will be expecting a brief no later than forty-eight hours on this matter," Director Young said then walked off.

"You guys are getting to blow up one day, I can just see it." Flynn expressed her prediction, once Young was out of earshot.

"Yeah when we do, I just hope the fella have a good game like he talks," Spencer retorted then walked off to begin investigating the crime. Agent Flynn walked the opposite way and headed over to the Wawa gas station rooftop. Where she saw everything just how Director Young had acted it out. *This shit is crazy.*

* * *

IT WAS an hour before dawn and Ayesha had been listening to Detective Eastwood tell her all about her father's investigation of his murder, and yet still hadn't convinced Ayesha of a logical reason of why him and his partner had stop pursuing the murdera. He was grateful for his family to be in Utah visiting family on his wife, Emily's side. He wasn't sure how impassive Ayesha would have been towards his three days aging from 3-8 years old. For hours, Eastwood had been handcuffed behind his back, sitting on the floor of his own living room. He knew exactly who Ayesha was, and now knew who was responsible for the recent murders lately, where the victims had crimson lipstick on their lips. Because he was now one of them wearing the same lipstick.

"So, let me sum this up, ..." Ayesha said while sitting on the edge of Eastwood's sofa, with her .9mm in her hand.

"My father and his protégé gets murdered, and his neighbors from DC come in and take his lead and y'all don't go after them like y'all wanted Tommy Gun? That's the most biased investigation I'd ever seen Eastwood-"

"Ayesha, we had no choice. No one would talk to us!" Eastwood exploded.

"What about the Pimptress that witnesses claimed to be close to my dad. Why didn't you guys go question her?" Ayesha stood off the sofa standing akimbo while looking down at Eastwood. Eastwood had no explanation for Ayesha that could possibly assuage her grief. And not land a bullet in his head. To keep Ayesha from blowing up, Eastwood sighed then told her the confidential truth.

"At the time, Ariel was assisting us to bring down your father, though the FBI had taken the case over. When your father was killed, we had no interest in her, and couldn't build a solid case on her ... so we gave up on her. Also, the night your father and Quavis was killed, Ariel was wearing a wire! ... so, we knew where she was on the night of the murder," Eastwood explained.

"So, the Pimptress was ready to hand my daddy over, huh?" Ayesha asked.

"Yes, Ayesha she—"

Psst! Psst! Psst! ... Before Eastwood could finish, Ayesha pulled the trigger and emptied the clip on Eastwood.

"Thanks for your cooperation," Ayesha said then exited the home inconspicuously.

This murder was different from her previous murders … She left behind a present for Camilla, that she would gladly appreciate. With a smile on her face as she rode through traffic gingerly, Ayesha was proud of her progress. She would have never thought in a million years that the Pimptress was conspiring to set her father up.

I could only imagine how many more motherfuckers like her was standing behind my daddy stabbing him in his back, Ayesha thought then thought of her next victim. Bad as she wanted Ariel, Ayesha had other plans that served its purpose.

CHAPTER 15

"*D*amn son, somebody really tryna knock that racist ass Ben Scott off the map. If I had to guess, McCarthy got some real goons out there," Boss said to Young Zoe who was in a daze staring out the limousine's back window thinking about Ayesha. The news of Arnold Bush being assassinated was global and had a lot of political officials worried. Young Zoe, being fond of politics himself, tried to weed through the mystery and agreed with everyone else. *McCarthy has some real bold goons,* Young Zoe thought as the limousine pulled into his condo complex in South Philly.

"I think the man doing us all a favor ... shit, we don't need that cracka Ben Scott in the White House that's for certain," Young Zoe said to Boss.

"So, what's on yo' mind about Bianca ... did you know she was kicking it with the boy?" Boss asked Young Zoe concerning Breezy.

"She's been known to fuck with them niggas so it's not a surprise. It's just now will she be an issue, is the catch-22. Back then, we ain't know shit about prostitution and the benefits of it. So, we left Ariel alone and let her do her. She built that bitch into a goldmine bro, and Bianca turned it into straight diamonds. The bitch got an army like us ... is it time to war or play it smooth?" Young Zoe explained to Boss who was stuck between the same hard rock as him. Going to war meant to abandon his world tour and risk a new hot rapper emerging, and stealing the light from him. So, Young Zoe knew that he had to make a smart decision, and handle the situation like a boss would.

"We not going to sign our names on Breezy's murder. Today, I'mma drop a rest in peace track. Let's remember we can't get clumpsy Fat Boy —"

"So, what about Bianca? I don't trust that ho, for real son," Boss interrupted while removing his Gucci shades from his eyes.

"Fuck Bianca ... if she gets stupid, then we'll get stupid, but until then we gonna remain cool, Boss," Young Zoe advised his right-hand man, who was ready to go to war with the North Philly cats. Young Zoe knew that Boss wasn't liking the play, but there wasn't shit Boss could do about it. To override Young Zoe would be total disrespect and cause friction between the two partners.

"I just hope we making a right choice, homie," Boss stated.

"We are, just chill and let shit cool down," Young Zoe said, then stepped out the limousine, immediately surrounded by his entourage.

"About Ayesha ... I'm still waiting on shorty to hit me up. When she do, I'mma see if I could put you in the car with one of her cousins," Young Zoe said to Boss. The smile that appeared on Boss' face revealed that he was liking that idea.

"Now that sounds like a plan, all them bitches beautiful," Boss retorted with a smile on his face.

"Get up witcha later son," Young Zoe said as he gave Boss a bump on his fist.

"See ya son ... make sure you lay that track like gold, nigga."

"You already know I'mma do that," Young Zoe said then closed the door.

* * *

AYESHA, found it intriguing how she was learning the political warfare ... she called it the flip side to politics. She was learning it like everyone else, that she'd assassinated another Governor from the

Republication party. Ayesha had just stepped out of the steaming hot shower when her mind went back to the box Young Zoe had delivered to her.

I bet he thinks I'm so rude, I need to give the man a call and stop being so shy, Ayesha thought as she dried off with a fresh towel. Ayesha walked into her bedroom and quickly slid into sexy lingerie. She then rubbed cocoa butter lotion on her body.

"Fuck!" Ayesha exclaimed, realizing that she'd forgotten to shave her legs in the shower. She made a mental note to shave next time she took a shower, then slid into a pair of sexy cotton boy shorts and a belly expose t-shirt. She was exhausted from her mission and side project, and just wanted a decent time for sleep – without any interruptions. Ayesha closed her drapes then climbed into bed with her TV remote controller. She flipped through a couple channels and settled on the Disney Channel.

"Aww Mulan!" Ayesha exclaimed when she saw her favorite female heroine appearing in cartoon. She'd loved the Mulan since childhood and still had her complete bedroom setup of Mulan. *I remember when daddy brought me home the entire bed set, Alexis wanted to copy me,* Ayesha thought with a smile on her face. The thought down memory lane made Ayesha grab her cordless phone resting on her nightstand. As she went to dial Alexis' number, she found herself dialing (717) 605-4327.

"I can't believe 'em doing this," Ayesha said as she listened to the phone ring. She was about to disregard the call when the party answered the phone, with music in the background.

"Hello?"

Hearing his smooth, delicate voice seemed like a dream to Ayesha and caused her stomach to form with butterflies. For a moment she remained speechless, until he spoke again.

"What's up, ma? Ain't no need to play the mouse game, did you like them roses and candy?" Young Zoe asked already knowing when the unfamiliar number was. Ayesha felt like a child and wanted to hang up, but thought it would be too childish.

"How do you know this is me, and not one of your regular booty calls?" Ayesha broke the ice and got an immediate chuckle from Young Zoe.

Damn he has a sexy ass laugh.

"First, I don't have any regular booty calls, and I don't go around giving every girl of my interest roses and candy, let alone a beautiful teddy bear," Young Zoe retorted causing Ayesha to smile and gratify being special in his eyes.

"You're smooth I gotta give that to you —"

"It's nothing I have to rehearse, I just gotta be me, Ayesha," Young Zoe retorted. The way he said her name made her moist between the legs. *Damn, he says my name with so much affection!* Ayesha thought as she slid a pillow between her legs to control herself.

"How did you locate me ... and what is it that you remember about me. I don't remember you at all, but I know for fact that you were signed to my daddy's label —"

"And I turned out to be the man I wouldn't be without yo' father. A lot of niggas fell off, but I continued to take off and regulate with his winners," Young Zoe retorted.

"Damn that's some real shit, but who are these winners, because what I'm hearing some DC niggas took over all my daddy possessions. Is that who killed my daddy?" Ayesha asked Young Zoe.

"That's an insult, baby ... the DC niggas got mad love for your dad and until this day they worship Tommy Gun. If a nigga from DC played grimy, Young Zoe would've been bodied that nigga ... so don't believe what you hear," Young Zoe explained to Ayesha, diminishing all thoughts of DC niggas possibly having a hand in Tommy Gun's murder.

"If you ask me who killed Tommy Gun, I'll tell you somebody who wanted him out the way, and thought that they'll be able to take over his empire. But they mis-calculated Ayesha, the soldiers that were holding yo' daddy down stood firm —"

Ayesha was hearing everything Young Zoe was filling her head with and it only brought her almost back to square one with the hunt for her daddy's killer. She wanted to probe Young Zoe further, but she decided to change the subject and keep her interest of finding her father's killer under the radar.

"It's nice of you to send me roses and the candy … and the teddy bear. What's unique is the candy. How'd you know that I would love them?"

Young Zoe chuckled briefly.

"Let's just say I remember a time ago when yo' daddy sent me to the dollar store in his Rolls Royce to pick up a specific brand of candy. It stuck with me, because I ended up doing it a couple more times," Young Zoe explained.

"That's cute —"

"So are you, and it's blowing my mind that I'm actually talking with you. You just don't know how glad I'm that you decided to call," Young Zoe said to Ayesha. She could hear the excitement he was bridling in his voice and it made her see a different principle about herself. *He's a famous man, and I am just the daughter of a legendary that's been dead for ten years. And he's blushing his ass off,* Ayesha thought. She didn't know what made her say it so soon but it surprised her as much as it surprised him.

"I want to see you."

"All you get to do is tell me when, Ma," Young Zoe retorted.

"Come by my place in an hour," Ayesha said.

"'Em coming, Ma," Young Zoe said to a dead line, for Ayesha was already gone.

On any other occasion, Young Zoe wouldn't have stepped out the recording booth for no one until he was done with his truck. He was a business-minded rapper and went off the principle: Money before fame and pressure. Today he was breaking them rules, not wanting to pass up a chance with Ayesha. A woman that's been on his mind since meeting her in New York, and a woman he was glad that he didn't kill ten years ago. From an honest perspective, Young Zoe saw all kinds of innocence, and it was mainly the reason why Ayesha was still alive today. He had no stomach to kill an innocent child. But he had enough dick to kill some pussy the way he was feeling at the moment.

Young Zoe could hear the call for sex in Ayesha's voice transparently. And all he could think of as the limousine inched its way closer to Ayesha's vicinity is how good her womanhood was. *Damn, I can't believe she really called me and is inviting me over,* Young Zoe thought as his driver Mac came to a red light at an intersection. Young Zoe badly wanted to get on the phone and brag to Boss that his dream had finally came true. But he knew that Boss deep down felt that he was making a mistake, and that messing with Ayesha wasn't a bright idea.

Fuck what he thinks, she was a little girl and we were ski masked up in that bitch, Young Zoe thought as a flashback of the night he shot Tommy Gun invaded his thoughts. He remembered seeing Ayesha hugging onto her daddy and the explosion from Tommy Gun's head splatter in blood and brains onto the face of nine-year-old Ayesha.

Damnit, the fuck did she have to be there, man?! Young Zoe thought as he shook his head to get rid of the memory. But as much as he tried, the memory was indelible, and was a night that changed his life and status from menace to Boss. *"Youngin" will always be a part of me until the day I die,* Young Zoe thought as Mac pulled off on the green light. Five minutes later, Mac was pulling into Ayesha's condo complex and parked behind Ayesha's all black .745.

"Mac, make yourself at home, I'mma be awhile, keep ya ears and eyes open, big guy," Young Zoe said to Mac.

"I got you boss man, take yo' time," Mac retorted.

Young Zoe stepped out of the limo and immediately put on a pair of Marc Jacobs shades to fade the ardent sun beaming down from heaven. He then strutted up to Ayesha's condo. Before he could knock, the door came open, and he instantly became speechless and erect. Standing there was Ayesha in a sexy lingerie and Jason Wu Stilettos. Young Zoe looked at Ayesha's sexy legs and was turned on by the satin net stockings.

"For someone to be a rapper, he show stuck on what he want to spit. Or is it uncommon for a woman to be so bold at what she wants?" Ayesha asked Young Zoe, who was mesmerized at Ayesha's curvaceous body. With no words to respond, Young Zoe took action. He stepped into the condo with Ayesha, simultaneously placing his lips to hers and scooping her in his arms. Ayesha closed the door with a kick and held onto Young Zoe's strong neck.

Oh, my God ... it's going down! Ayesha thought as her heartbeat accelerated.

"Upstairs, first room ... on the right," Ayesha managed to direct Young Zoe through a storm of kisses. Like she'd directed, Young Zoe was moving up the stairs while kissing Ayesha slowly and passionately. It wasn't a one night stand kiss, and Ayesha took notice immediately. *It's like he's been waiting for this day for many years,* Ayesha thought as Young Zoe found her bedroom.

With the drapes being closed, the only illumination came from the TV that was on a low volume. Young Zoe laid Ayesha down on her bed and quickly began to remove his clothes. She watched him every step of the way and took in his sexy, muscular frame. She could tell by his brawny figure that he worked out frequently.

WOW! Ayesha thought as she stared at Young Zoe. When he removed his shades, and looked down at her, her stomach tightened and her heart begin racing. His eyes were on fire and burning with passion. Her body broke out with an excessive sweat. There was a familiarity about them that she couldn't recall.

"Damn, I know you ... you're the man for me, I remember you. You're the —"

Oh Shit! Young Zoe thought, a second away from panicking.

"One I'm scared of," Ayesha said seductively as she removed her satin see-through thong and held her leg up in the air.

She knows me! Young Zoe thought.

"Come take this pussy, but please let me remind you ... 'em not that little girl from ten years ago, so beat this —"

Before Ayesha could finish talking Young Zoe buried his face in her nice, shaven wet mound.

"Mmm ... yes Dayvon, eat this pussy!" Ayesha purred as she gyrated her hips, calling Young Zoe by his government name. The way she said Dayvon was music to Young Zoe's ears, and something that made him realize that Ayesha was different from what he called his fun bitches.

Ayesha's head was spinning in circles as Young Zoe ate her pussy like a pro. Every flick of his tongue sent electrifying waves of pleasure throughout her body. She could feel him everywhere, and it wasn't like Brandon had ever made her feel. When Young Zoe made her come to her first orgasm, he found his fitted jeans on the floor and retrieved a condom. Ayesha grabbed the condom, ripped it open, and put it in her mouth. She then grabbed Young Zoe's hand and pulled him onto the bed, then laid him on his back. Young Zoe watched Ayesha lick his throbbing dick then begin to suck him slow while the condom stayed in her mouth. When Ayesha was satisfied and ready to feel Young Zoe inside of her, she deep throated him, simultaneously sliding on the condom.

"Damn Ma ... you too much," Young Zoe purred.

Ayesha giggled like a college girl then climbed on top of him, straddling Young Zoe. Ayesha reached back behind her and guided Young Zoe's dick inside her wet mound. Slowly, she descended and exhaled soft moans as she lifted her love box up with all his length.

"Damn Dayvon, this dick fits all my needs," Ayesha whispered in Young Zoe's ear as she slowly rode him.

"And 'em glad to be able to accommodate you beautiful, I just don't want this to be a one-time thing —"

Oh, my God did he just say that?! Ayesha thought.

"It won't ... I promise you it won't," Ayesha purred then begin to kiss Young Zoe deeply.

"You're different Ma —"

"You too," Ayesha agreed with Young Zoe, who was hitting strong notes at the right time, and unbeknownst to him, changing Ayesha T. Jordan's perspective on relationships. If she ever tried, she felt safe to try it with Young Zoe, a man that knew her before she knew herself. *Damn, he's so damn fine and knows how to open me up for real,* Ayesha thought as she came to an electrifying orgasm again.

"Ooohh shit, Dayvon!" she shouted as her body convulsed, and her eyes rolled behind her head like never before.

* * *

THE EASTWOOD'S residence was the breaking news and the only talk on the 5 o'clock afternoon news. It was a shocking to everyone that knew Michael Eastwood. Camilla, herself, had found her partner's gruesome state when he didn't show up at the precinct for work, nor answered any of her concerned calls. When she pulled up and saw his unmarked SUV parked in the driveway, she immediately thought that he'd overslept, until she knocked on the door and found it ajar. She saw her partner's bloody body sprawled on the living room floor. It took her to control every muscle in her body to not vomit. Though it was her partner inside the house dead, she was wrapped in bewilderment, trying to figure out how his murder was linked to the two previous murder victims, who'd also had a crimson coat of lipstick on their lips. Camilla was standing outside writing a witness report when Detectives Cranmer and Lindsey pulled up in an unmarked SUV. The case had been assigned to them immediately by the Chief, when he'd learned of the lipstick involvement. Crime scene investigators, K9 unit, and other detectives were all over the place looking for evidence that would lead to the killer. A moment later, after they'd pulled up, Camilla embraced herself as her two co-workers approached her.

"Camilla ... I'm so sorry that this has happened," Cranmer said as he hugged Camilla expressing his consolation. She tried everything not to break down, but it was too fresh and the sight of Eastwood was still behind her eye lids.

"We're gonna find this bastard, Camilla," Lindsey promised while rubbing Camilla's back offering her support.

"They killed him in cold blood while in handcuffs, he never had a chance ..." Camilla paused to gain control of her emotions. She pulled away from Cranmer and wiped her tears away. Her makeup was ruined, and she was a compete wreck.

"The killer left a lipstick behind after applying it on his lips," Camilla informed Cranmer and Lindsey.

"Do we have any witnesses?"

"None," Camilla told Cranmer.

"Do you think Eastwood knows the killer?" Lindsey asked.

"No forced entrance, and all the windows were locked. Look like the killer walked right through the front door," Camilla explained.

"Come," Camilla said then led Cranmer and Lindsey inside the house.

As soon as they entered, Cranmer and Lindsey saw their co-worker's body underneath a white shroud. Cranmer knelt down and pulled back the shroud. He wasn't looking for the cause of death, he only had one interest on his mind.

The lipstick, what the hell does it mean? Cranmer thought as he stared at Eastwood's crimson colored lips, and only his lips.

"Lindsey?" Cranmer called out to his partner while still staring at Eastwood's lips.

"Yes," Lindsey answered.

"I think we're looking at a serial killer … however, this could be a connection to Raekon and Tony. But then it could also be the killer's signature," Cranmer explained as he stood and looked around the room.

"No struggle, he either knew the killer or trusted that the killer wasn't a threat," Lindsey considered.

"I'll agree with that one," Cranmer retorted, then knelt back down and picked up an empty .9mm shell casing.

"Same model as the others, we'll know tomorrow if it's fired from the same weapon," said Cranmer.

"Trust me … it's a match," Lindsey retorted.

Both detectives turned their head and saw Camilla making a hastened departure from the chilling scenery inside.

"She's taking this hard, Cranmer."

"I know … I don't think that neither of us with our training experience, or anybody else, could imagine what she's going through," Cranmer retorted.

"I feel sorry for her."

"She'll be okay after a couple of days, until then, 'em looking for the son of a bitch that killed our friend," Cranmer said, very determined at finding the killer.

CHAPTER 16

*J*t's been two days since she had the time of her life with Young Zoe, and ever since then they'd been on the phone, unable to get enough of each other. Young Zoe was on tour in Newark, New Jersey, and wouldn't be back in Philadelphia until two weeks. It was unusual for Ayesha to crave any man's affection; so, it was all new to her. After giving Alexis and Tamara an ear full of her exclusive time with Young Zoe, both of her cousins agreed that she was sprung. And bad as she didn't want to admit it, she saw the signs as well. To get a fresh scenery for a change, Ayesha decided to get out of her condo and go shopping. It was time for her to upgrade on everything, clothes, shoes, heels, and some new wheels. She'd caught the train to North Philadelphia and walked a block to a Porsche car dealership, getting crazy looks from employees and some customers, immediately. *These motherfuckers think a black bitch sleep walking, huh?* Ayesha thought, then asked one middle-aged woman who was checking out a badass Porsche.

"Do you have a problem … or is it that we know each other from somewhere?"

The lady looked at Ayesha, then looked around, putting on an act as if she didn't think Ayesha was talking to her.

Here goes this Hollywood shit, Ayesha thought.

"See, I hate it when y'all bitches do that shit," Ayesha said with attitude then rolled her eyes. "Yeah bitch 'em talking to your bad acting ass" Ayesha retorted.

"Excuse me ma'am, but last time I checked this was America, and I'm free to look where the hell I darn please —"

"Excuse me ladies. Um Patty, Michelle is waiting for you to make your monthly payment," the manager said to the woman, steering her away from Ayesha and towards a representative's office. Unbeknownst to Patty, she was just a moment away from getting her old white ass, ghetto beat.

"And ma'am, sorry for the inconvenience, but how may I accommodate you at *Porsches For You?*" the manager asked Ayesha.

"I'm here to buy the best Porsche on this lot, and please don't ask me if I can afford it. I'm not here to pay monthly payments, sir ... I'm her to buy and own," Ayesha informed the manager, who was indeed skeptical of Ayesha, but quickly cast his judgement away and put on his business face.

"Well, I'm here to tell you that you've come to the right place, young lady ... come and let me show you what looks like you," said the manager then led Ayesha outside the building, and to a line of luxury Porsches of a variety of colors.

Ayesha took a look at all the nice Porsches and loved them all. It took her an hour to finally settle on a pearl white Porsche Carrera 67 with all-white, rich leather seats and wood grain interior. When she sat in the driver's seat, she just knew that it was what she needed.

"This me, Toby, don't you think?" Ayesha asked the manager she'd became acquainted with over the last hour.

"It's you all day, baby girl," Toby retorted with both hands in the pockets of his Brioni slacks.

"I want it," said Ayesha as she took in the comfort of the leather seats.

"Ms. Jordan, this car is running $300,000, and just to release it you'll need $100,000 —"

"You must ain't her me an hour ago. I don't want payments, I'm here to buy, Toby. Now I need the keys and the papers to this car, please," Ayesha requested.

"Okay, let me get all the paperwork ready," Toby said then pulled out his cellular phone and dialed his secretary.

"Yeah um, Sandy, um we're releasing a Porsche Carrera GT. Can you get the paperwork ready for me, and the keys as well ... this is a buy," Toby informed his secretary. "Okay Sandy thank you," Toby said then wrapped up his call.

"It's all yours, now let's do numbers," Toby informed Ayesha.

"Now I like the sound of that," Ayesha retorted, then followed Toby inside to transfer the $300,000 from an off seas account in Barbuda. The process took precisely thirty minutes for the money to clear, then a couple signatures, and the keys were Ayesha's.

As she drove off the lot, she burnt rubber, leaving a storm of smoke behind, feeling like a new Ayesha. From time to time during the following hours of her shopping, she checked her iPhone numerous of times, expecting to see "Young Zoe" pop up. But he never called, and it made her realize how much she was longing for him.

Damn that nigga got me hooked ... I need to really get myself together, Ayesha thought while walking through the North Philly mall.

It wasn't until she'd seen the white man in the business suit trail her after shopping at three clothes stores that she realized that she had company. Ayesha walked into another clothing store and walked down an aisle, pretending to be an interested customer. She stopped at a shelf and with her peripheral vision, she saw the man appear at the end of the aisle. Ayesha abruptly turned towards the man and walked in his direction. Before she could get in his reach, the man strutted off and walked on the next aisle. Ayesha followed and caught him pretending to be interested in a pair of Polo shirts. Ayesha came up and stood next to the man in the suit and shades with her bags in her hand.

"Who sent you, you're such a poor trailer?" Ayesha asked the man, surprising him. He smiled briefly then whispered to Ayesha.

"For hours, you've been receiving a call, and your phone isn't with you."

Oh shit, 'em trippin'. I left the track phone at home. I never do that shit! Ayesha thought.

"'Em so sorry —"

"Don't be sorry, just be available in the next hour, it is very important," the man in the suit said, then walked off in a hurry.

"Shit," Ayesha exclaimed, then made a quick departure from the mall.

Being on call meant being available when she was needed, something that the Master had told her was very important. A missed call was like a failed mission, and a failed mission could lead you to termination. And the only termination that Ayesha could receive from her superiors was death, unbeknownst to Ayesha.

It was precisely forty-five minutes later when Ayesha pulled up to her condo and parked next to her .745. She grabbed her shopping bags, then hurried inside her condo. Ayesha dropped her bags on the sofa, and made a dash upstairs to her bedroom. Once inside her bedroom, she heard her Verizon track phone ringing on her nightstand. Ayesha quickly snatched up the phone and answered.

What the hell happened to an hour?

"Hello?!"

"Please enter your code name please" *–Beep!*

Murderlicious— Ayesha typed in her code name quickly.

"Thank you, please wait for your representative," said the automated voice, then put Ayesha on hold with Jazz music playing in the background.

Ayesha sat on the bed and patiently waited for the line to clear. As she waited, she noticed that the redolence of Young Zoe's cologne still lingered, and made her replay their night in her room all over again. Looking towards her bedroom door, she imagined that Young Zoe had suddenly appeared, and was coming to give her body another night of affection.

Damn this nigga really got my head going places it shouldn't be going, Ayesha thought then noticed the moisture forming between her legs.

"WOW!" Ayesha exclaimed then crossed her legs to gain control of herself. *That nigga still haven't called me,* Ayesha thought the line was cleared.

"Murderlicious?" her representative called out for assurance.

"Yes, this is me," Ayesha retorted.

"Good listen, Florida in Martin County, Stuart is the city. 1204 SE Ocean Blvd. His name is Willie Spruce. Now there's something different that needs to happen here, Murderlicious—"

"Okay, I'm listening," Ayesha informed her representative taking a mental note of all the information he was giving her.

"We need you to leave your signature."

"What do you mean?" Ayesha asked perplexed not knowing what signature he needed her to leave on a crime scene.

"The lipstick signature."

What the fuck? How do he know about what I've been doing to my victims? Ayesha thought extremely surprised, that it had her speechless.

"Don't worry, Murderlicious, your work will always be safe with your superiors," Ayesha's representative said then disconnected the call.

Ayesha couldn't believe how much her superiors knew of her, it was as if she was being watched 24/7.

"Who the hell are these people?" Ayesha stated amongst herself looking dumbfounded. The news had only declared to the Philadelphian's that a serial killer branding victims with lipstick was in the area. *Never did they say that they knew of serial killer identity... So how could my superiors know?* Ayesha thought, then prepared to leave for Florida. *They wanted me to leave my signature in the Sunshine State ... the homeland if Jimmy McCarthy. WOW!* Ayesha thought as her adrenaline increased with her eagerness to meet her next target.

* * *

IT WAS A MATTE BRAND, and continued DNA from Raekon Adams and Tony McQueen, as well as Eastwood's. *A fuckin' crimson lipstick, what does it mean?* Detective Cranmer thought while reading the lab report on the results of the lipstick found on Eastwood's crime scene. He was sitting at his desk trying to piece together what transparently was a puzzle, when he looked up he saw Detective Lindsey walking into the office with a two steaming Styrofoam cups of coffee. She handed Cranmer a cup then took a seat in the chair in front of his desk.

"Thank you, Christina," Cranmer said politely.

"You're welcome … so what's the news?" Lindsey asked seeing that Cranmer was reading a lab report.

"DNA from Raekon and Tony was found on the lipstick and the .9mm shell matches the rest of them," Cranmer said then took a sip of his coffee. When he put his cup back down and looked at his partner holding her cup in both hands, he espied the lipstick print on Lindsey's cup and was hit with a disturbing prospect.

"What is it Cranmer?" Lindsey asked when she saw the look on Cranmer's face.

"Do you think this killer could be a female?" Cranmer asked while still staring at the lipstick print on Lindsey's cup.

"Well if we go back to the unidentified woman on the video surveillance at Raekon's scene. All we know is no other body entered the hotel room, unless — "

"They came through the window," Cranmer considered, after remembering the facts of Raekon's murder.

"The killer had a chance to enter and exit from the window. But that means that the killer had to enter into another room. I remember the stairs only covering two floors outside the window," Cranmer said, then took another sip of his coffee.

"So, it is possible that the killer had a room either on the fourth or third floor, and made their way up to Raekon's room, entering by the window?" Cranmer asked.

"Cranmer..." Lindsey said as she stood and placed her cup on Cranmer's desk.

"I just can't see no female going through all that trouble to climb through a window and kill Raekon. A man's capabilities are overwhelming in both cases," Lindsey gave her opinion.

"So why do you think both Raekon and Tony were naked?"

"Maybe it's when the killer caught them...when they were naked," Lindsey retorted.

She has a point, Cranmer thought then looked back at Lindsey's cup and at the lipstick print on the rim of her cup. But there's something we're not getting in this entire picture. *Why the hell does the killer leave behind a lipstick that contains DNA from the murder victims?* Cranmer thought then looked up at Lindsey who was playing with her nails.

"Do you think the killer left the lipstick on purpose?"

"Acourse, he did," Lindsey retorted sticking to her belief that the killer was a man.

"We're going to find him," Cranmer retorted accepting Lindsey's theory that the killer was a man.

* * *

THE R.I.P. HIT that Young Zoe had just released an hour ago was an insult to Trouble, and Bianca. The death of their true friend was still troubling them. Every night since Breezy's death, Trouble and his North Philly comrades had been committed to driveby shootings, and were unsatisfied because they were hitting less than they'd intended to. The South Philly cats were always expecting the heat and were already in position. When Trouble received the call from Bianca that a couple of cats were slipping at the salon on 76th and Kanner, he moved quickly and called up his homie Toetag, who everyone knew in North Philly as a marksman.

Toetag hated South Philly cats, and despised Young Zoe with a passion. When Trouble's driver Kane pulled up the salon a block away, Trouble saw the activity. Darkness had just fallen, and the prostitutes and hustlers where moving around, going about their professions. Trouble and Toetag looked at the block meticulously, making sure that they weren't walking into a death trap.

"They sleeping, son," Toetag said while clutching his Mac10 in the backseat sitting behind Trouble who was riding shotgun. Toetag despite his five-foot-four height and 145 pounds, was a man who was always ready to lay a nigga down.

"Let me call shorty and see where she at," Trouble retorted then dialed Bianca's number. Bianca's phone rung twice before her delicate voice spilled through the receiver.

"What's up, Trouble?"

"Yo, we out here, where these niggas at?" Trouble asked Bianca.

"They're in an apartment next to the salon, when you go in two bitches will be with them. Please don't do shit to my hoes Trouble, the door will be unlocked," said Bianca.

"I got you, now which apartment?"

"Apartment #102," Bianca retorted.

"Appreciate you, B."

"No problem, make it rain on them niggas," Bianca retorted then hung up the phone.

"Kane, pull up to that building next to the Salon and keep this bitch hot. Toetag we hitting everything except the ho's son," Trouble ordered.

"Let's do this shit," Toetag retorted then pulled down his ski mask over his face. Trouble followed suit as Kane pulled off and pulled up to the curb in front of the apartment building.

Trouble and Toetag quickly made an exit and into the apartment swaying their guns at prostitutes and fiends who occupied the apartment buildings. The hustlers a couple buildings down had no clue what was going down in their own backyard. Trouble and Toetag took the stairs and covered them in hurry.

When they came to the landing, Trouble led the way and made a dash down the hall. Before Trouble made it to apartment #102 the door opened. Trouble aimed and was a second away from pulling the trigger, until he saw the prostitute stick her head out. When she saw the gunman, she was startled and about to scream, until Trouble shoved his Glock .40 into her mouth.

"Bitch, back into the trap, and don't think about screaming, do you hear me?" Trouble told the prostitute who nodded her head in agreement.

Trouble removed the gun and pushed the prostitute back into the apartment. When Trouble and Toetag entered the apartment the distinctive cries of moans could be heard coming from the backroom.

"How many?" Trouble asked the prostitute.

"Two, they only wanted my friend— " Before Tina Bell could get her next words out, Trouble took off towards the back room down a dimly lit hallway.

"Mmm mmm," the moans of the prostitute emanated from the room. Trouble found the door ajar and peeped in catching sight of the threesome in action. Two men were having a good time with the prostitute, who was being fucked from the back and simultaneously sucking the other man's dick. Trouble looked at Toetag then kicked the door open.

"Oh shit," the man getting his dick sucked shouted as he saw the two masked men invading.

The man whose back was turned never had a chance. Trouble's Glock .40 barked, nailing him in the back of his head, sending blood and brains on the screaming prostitute. Toetag shot the second startled man right between his eyes and watched him slide down the wall lifeless. The screaming prostitute covered herself with the bloody sheets and embraced herself for the shots to hit her next. Trouble badly wanted to take her out to stop from waking up the neighbors, but his orders from the Pimptress were strictly. Trouble and Toetag left the apartment and made it to their getaway successfully, leaving two of Boss' men from his drug operation dead.

CHAPTER 17

When Ayesha arrived in Florida, she was excited to learn that Young Zoe was visiting the Sunshine State as well. He was scheduled to perform at a night club in Tampa, Florida called "Club Sky." It was an enormous popular club that celebrities attended every weekend. When Ayesha informed Young Zoe that she would be passing through Tampa on a trip to visit a family member. Young Zoe immediately offered her to come hang out with him while he represented Philadelphia. It was an offer that Ayesha just couldn't pass up for nothing in the world. When Ayesha pulled into the hotel parking lot she espied Young Zoe's tour bus and some of his men, from his entourage. When the men saw Ayesha pearl white Porsche pull in behind Young Zoe's limousine they all looked on in awe. Bone, the head man of Young Zoe's entourage had been expecting Ayesha's arrival. As Ayesha was stepping out the car Bone approached her while the other men looked on.

"Ayesha glad that you could make it, if you don't mind I will escort you to the tour bus." Bone said to Ayesha trying his best to control his manhood while looking at Ayesha in the skin tight mini dress; she had on accentuating her curvaceous body. Bone was from the DC area and Ayesha could distinguish the accent remarkably.

"That'll be fine with me, just as long as I get to him in one piece," Ayesha responded.

"Trust me Ma, you're in good hands. They don't call me Bone just for the hell of it. I'll break a nigga face, before they come two feet towards you, Ma. Now please let me get you there safely," Bone said then offered his arm for Ayesha to intertwine.

This nigga is a real character, Ayesha thought, with a sexy smirk on her face then grabbed on to Bone's muscular arm.

"By the way, that's a nice Porsche you got yourself."

"Thanks, but it's not for sale," Ayesha said as her and Bone took off towards the tour bus.

Young Zoe was in conversation with Boss on his cell phone while laid back on the plush sofa when Ayesha and Bone stepped on the tour bus. Boss was furious about his men that were killed on 76th and Kanner, and felt that the niggas from North Philly were responsible.

"My nigga, we don't know who responsible, it could be some jealous ass cat who was trying to get them boyz out of the way. Who knows, but you can't act off of emotions, Boss. So, let's chill and see what is what, until then let me hit you back up, because I have company," Young Zoe informed Boss as he sat up and Ayesha sat on his lap.

"A'ight my nigga, do yo' thang tonight and call me if you need anybody mopped homeboy," Boss retorted.

"I got you, Boss," Young Zoe said then hung up the phone. Young Zoe tossed his phone on the other sofa and looked at Bone who was watching the flat screen TV, where a game of NFL Tampa Bay and Green Bay was displaying.

"Got her here in one piece," Boss said Bone.

"Appreciate that Bone make sure me and my friend have no interruptions," Young Zoe ordered Bone while he crossed Ayesha's smooth thighs as he held her from behind.

"I got you, Boss … give me a call when you need me." Bone said then made his departure.

"You really came, huh?" Young Zoe asked Ayesha who turned around and gave Young Zoe a slow passionate kiss.

"Why would I pass this opportunity up?" Ayesha said as she laid

Young Zoe back and climbed on top of him while rubbing on his muscular chest.

"So, what you see is an opportunity, that tells me your mind isn't made up —"

"Stop it, because if my mind wasn't made up I wouldn't be here when I could be with family," Ayesha said then kissed Young Zoe on his lips.

As the kiss intensified, Young Zoe slid his hands up Ayesha's mini dress and found her panty less, and wet between her legs when he felt her mound. Ayesha let out a soft mound then began snaking her tongue down Young Zoe's body. When she got to his navel Ayesha unfastened Young Zoe's belt and unzipped his jeans. Slowly she pulled out his throbbing dick and placed it in her mouth. As she sucked him slow, she looked into Young Zoe's eyes and melted like always when she made eye contact with him. There was definitely something familiar about his eyes to her, but she couldn't place her hands on any previous common ground.

"Damn Ma, you're so damn beautiful ..." Young Zoe complimented Ayesha as she continued to sex him with her mouth. Ayesha made a wet popping sound when she pulled his dick out of her mouth and began to stroke him.

"And you are a handsome ass nigga that I don't want to get caught up with," Ayesha responded while stroking Young Zoe.

"Why?"

"Because Dayvon ... I never allowed myself to get attached to no man."

Young Zoe pulled Ayesha by her hand, and made her straddle him. He then pulled up her mini dress over her head and tossed it on the floor.

"Being afraid is understandable baby. Not every man will treat a woman like her worth. I could have the world, but if I have to make a choice ..." Young Zoe said then grabbed Ayesha by her chin and forced her to look into his eyes. His look was sincere and the fire burning amongst them caused her to react like she'd never done to a man. Tears escaped her eyes revealing that she'd been broken.

"I choose you," Young Zoe said then attacked Ayesha's erected nipples.

"Mmm ... Dayvon!" Ayesha moaned out as she reached behind her and grabbed his dick. She didn't care about using any protection, today she was taking her chances, and claiming her man. Ayesha guided Young Zoe inside her wet mound and slowly descended on his shaft while Young Zoe continued to suck on her brown nipples. Their bodies became one synchronization with the both of them stepping over the line with mutual concordance, - they were made for each other.

* * *

LOSING two of his men just wasn't sitting right with Boss, and for Young Zoe to advise him to chill and not act on emotions, it bothered Boss. He could remember a time when Young Zoe would respond to the other side with nothing to think about. Boss felt like Young Zoe was changing on him dramatically.

It just wasn't like him to let a nigga get away with fucking over his men, Boss thought as he sat in his living room on his plush sofa smoking a blunt; and flickering through the channels on his sixty-four flat screen TV. Boss took a pull from the blunt and exalted the smoke realizing that the fame and money in the rap industry was causing his homie to lose focus.

We're both on two different planets, Boss thought while shaking his head. It was what made Young Zoe and him take Tommy Gun out, because Tommy Gun put himself above two young niggas with a different mindset than others. They were rappers and Tommy Gun was the kingpin; someone that they wanted to be. So, we came up with a plan to erase Tommy Gun's era and take over. Never did we plan to step higher than the other, so why do I have to be in my emotions when it's time to bust our guns back at our enemies.

"Fuck that shit Youngin', we made a pack to always ride with each other. Not ain't the time to lay down," Boss exclaimed as he dialed up Taz on his iPhone.

We been knockin' these niggas off and we gonna continue! Boss thought.

"Hello?" Taz answered.

"We moving on hunti-em down, I need you and Mane on this one," Boss ordered Taz.

"I got you bossman," Taz retorted.

"DC style, homie," Boss said then hung up the phone going against Young Zoe's suggestion to chill.

"Chilling and beef has always been like oil and water, Youngin'. I just hope not going soft on me," Boss said then took a long drag on his blunt when he looked at the TV he saw that he had it on BET and that Young Zoe's music video "Player" was displaying. It was a player's anthem, and Boss loved it like everyone else. He turned the volume up on the TV and sung along with Young Zoe.

"(insert music note) Fool's get tricked by looks, a good nookie never wink back/A real player say he took that/Ballers getting' full off cat/The stroke game got 'em hooked like crack/Young Zoe keep 'em coming back/?" Boss sung along while looking at all the pretty women in the video sporting the finest bikinis, and regretted giving up the rap game.

"I let a nigga determine my fuckin' future!" Boss exploded as he hurtled the remote controller at the TV.

The cats standing on 12th and Huntingdon at the corner store ran by Arabs were doing their usual late-night hustling. The Stentorian train vibrated the pavement as it coasted through the hood. It also allowed Taz and Mane to seize the opportunity to creep up on the cats shooting dice on the side of the Arab store. One of the cats saw Taz and Mane creeping and shouted in panic, but couldn't be heard due to the Stentorian train drowning his vocals out. Taz quickly aimed at the man while gaping and squeezed off two rounds from his Glock .40 nailing the man in his mouth artistically. The other cats were shot down by Mane as they scrambled for safety to no avail. Mane's M-16 drilled eight of them on the side of the store. Two managed to bend the corner and Taz took off after them. When he neared the corner, he found one on the ground clutching his wounds to his stomach, and the other man entering the Arab store.

"Please man, let me live I have kids man!" The man on the ground begged Taz as he stood over him aiming his Glock .40 at him.

"I know you got kids, and they all go to heaven," Taz said, then pulled the trigger hitting the man in his face with the remaining of his clip. Taz then released the empty clip, quickly inserted a fresh one, then took off with Mane. He hated leaving behind the man who'd managed to escape inside the store. But Taz was too street smart to walk into a death trap. It was all a part of the game, those who died by the gunfire and those who managed to escape the gunfire. Taz and Mane made it to their getaway and caught the ass end of the train just in time to also make a great escape.

* * *

AYESHA WAS ENJOYING the back stage VIP party with Young Zoe. There were beautiful women all over the place wearing next to nothing. A few of them would be taking the stage with Young Zoe and perform their amazing dance performance. They were his personal dancers, and Ayesha couldn't help but think of how many had he fucked behind the scenes, and on his tour bus. Despite her crazy thoughts, it was evident that she was the eye candy in VIP, and that's all that mattered other than knowing that Young Zoe was her man. Ayesha sat on the leather sofa with Young Zoe and allowed him to feed her a bowl of variety of fruits. He treated her queenly and she was appreciating the affection he showed her in front of his fans.

I can't believe his has happen so fast, Ayesha thought as she ate the purple grapes Young Zoe placed in her mouth.

"Are you enjoying yourself?" Young Zoe asked Ayesha. She sat intertwine with him with her legs crossed inhaling his Polo cologne, trying to control herself, lady like.

"I'm having a wonderful tie baby ... I just hate the fact that I have to leave after you perform," Ayesha explained to Young Zoe.

After getting to learn more about each other, Ayesha had lied to Young Zoe about her employment when he'd asked what it was that she did for a living. Ayesha flat out told Young Zoe that she was a company promoter for a company in New York, who went around the world promoting business offers to other companies dealing with computer data. When asked did she love her job, Ayesha praised her job with enthusiasm. The last thing he would ever expect was for Ayesha to be a superb lethal assassin.

"Don't worry Ma, you're only departing for a moment not forever baby," Young Zoe said to Ayesha then gave her a kiss on her lips.

"I'm gonna be lovesick again," Ayesha retorted.

"You're not alone … we will be in contact baby."

"I know we will baby, when you get back to Philly, I want to take you to meet my two cousins—"

"The two who were at the club with you when you broke ol' boy off?" Young Zoe asked recalling the time when Ayesha broke the NFL player name Craig's wrist for trying to shine one her.

"Baby that's not funny, that nigga tried putting down on me like I was his bitch or something. I wasn't with that —"

"So, you ninja chopped his ass," Young Zoe said then burst into laughter. Young Zoe's head man of his entourage, Bone, walked up to Young Zoe and handed him his mic.

"It's time boss, everybody waiting on you," Bone informed Young Zoe.

"Well beautiful, I gotta go put on for South Philly. First, Bone make sure you get her safely to the front row," Young Zoe said as he stood and pulled Ayesha in his arms. He kissed her deep and palmed her succulent ass. The kiss lasted every bit of a minute; that neither wanted to end.

"See you in a few," Young Zoe said then put on his Gucci shades.

"I'mma be there now go before you delay your other fans," Ayesha said.

Young Zoe took off with his entourage except Bone who jostled through the crunk crowd, getting Ayesha to the front row area. When Young Zoe came out on the stage he immediately turned the place out. As he performed Ayesha couldn't help but be self-effacing when Young Zoe performed his hit single "You Mines Now," the lyrics to the song was in concordance with what both of them knew for sure. And that was that the two of them now had in each other.

"From the sandbox watch you grow/I waited my time like a developed mango/Now it's our time to shine/baby girl you mines/not for tonight, tomorrow, but forever you be my lady/!" Young Zoe as he sung the lyrics looked at an exhilarating Ayesha who knew that the words were meant only for her."

Yes, baby I'm yours boo! Ayesha thought while listening to Young Zoe pour his heart out to her. *It's amazing how people can communicate through music,* Ayesha thought then blew her man a big kiss.

* * *

WHEN BIANCA HEARD of the news about the shooting that occurred on 12th and Huntingdon she, as well as Trouble, was furious. Young Zoe being on tour only told them that Boss had made the call. Bianca was ensconced with a millionaire client when Trouble called her with the news. It was one of her favorite clients who had a mansion in DC and treated her queenly. Despite his elderly age, he was in great shape at eighty-five years old, and could still get up naturally and last in the sack longer than most young men. Danny was an old-school Italian with a desire to marry beautiful Bianca.

For the third time he'd proposed to Bianca, and she'd only accepted an engagement ring worth 4.5 million dollars. Ever since the call she'd received from Trouble, Bianca had been deep in her thoughts. If there was any man to ever make her retire and who she'll elope with; it was Breezy. His death was still bothering her, in spite of their ephemeral relationship. *He was definitely a game changer,* Bianca thought as she laid in the canopy king sized bed, snuggled up against Danny's nice physique.

"Your mind is running a hundred miles per hour, Bianca," Danny spoke.

Bianca smiled then pulled the purple silk sheets up to her bosom and began rubbing Danny's eight pack stomach.

"There's a lot on my mind lately. I just don't understand the world sometimes. Why do the good die young, Danny?" Bianca asked.

"There's nothing to understand about life, in this world when we do we're only wrecking our brains woman," Danny spoke, in a resounding husky voice, while rubbing her bare back.

"What do you mean, Danny?" Bianca asked as she climbed on top of him and laid her head on his chest.

"The good die young because someone have to do bad, the same as if it was something like the beautiful sight of a baby being born. It's life, and for years it's been going on. That's why we must live life like we know we're dying tomorrow, and that's my forte," Danny explained.

He is so right ... I can't let Breezy life conflict mines, Bianca thought. Danny had no clue that he'd just gave Bianca advice to be more of a cold bitch. It was why I couldn't marry a man like you, because when the good fades away. I wouldn't have the heart to have any empathy. Bianca thought then slid down on Danny's erect shaft. What was unsaid in retort from her, Danny understood.

"Mmm! Mmm!" Bianca moaned out as she filled her love box with Danny's enormous size shaft. "My girth king!" Bianca complimented Danny on the girth of his shaft.

"My beautiful black queen," Danny retorted, then flipped Bianca onto her back never coming out of her love box. Danny tossed Bianca's sexy legs on his right shoulder and pounded her pussy rapidly and deep. Bianca could do nothing but gasp for air as she felt Danny's log teasing to enter her stomach.

"Damnit, Danny!" Bianca purred loudly after finding her voice.

It was the best fuck she'd had in a while and it was always when she came to DC to be with Danny. With the new advice on her mind from Danny, she now saw what he meant by living like you were dying tomorrow. And that's exactly what Danny was doing, Bianca realized, *fucking me like it was his last fuck!*

CHAPTER 18

*W*illie Spruce was a lean six-feet-three-inches, 210 pound German, and a journalist for the Stuart News. He was the best that the Stuart Newspaper had assessed in years, and was about to release to the world a scandalous secret about Democrat Presidential Governor McCarthy. The secret was sure to damage his chances of becoming the next President. But little did Willie know, McCarthy was already five moves ahead of him, and the right people were behind him. It was 5 o'clock p.m. when Willie and his coworker girlfriend Sandra walked out of their employment at Stuart News Press. Sandra was a gorgeous red head, freckle-faced twenty-four-year-old, who was in madly love with Willie, who'd only been dating Sandra for eight months. Her lean five-foot-three-inch figure was exquisite, and Willie was grateful to be the lucky man to have her. The duo walked to Willie's ocean blue .745 and held onto each other momentarily saying pleasant goodbyes like they did daily.

"Call me when you're done with the report Will," Sandra said to Willie while holding onto his waist and looking up to him. She wore heels daily and was fortunate for the boost of height it did give her at five inches. Willie leaned down and kissed Sandra once more on her pink, perky lips.

"Don't worry, you will be the first one to see it," Willie promised Sandra in reference of the scandalous secret he had on Governor McCarthy. She was like everyone else who'd learned that Willie was withholding information; desperate to hear it.

"If it's not the two love birds making out in the parking lot," Sandra's best friend Jessica said as she walked towards them heading for her car.

"Yes, it is, and we were just saying that steak and beer is due at your place this weekend right, Will?" Sandra said then looked up at Willie.

"Yep," Willie cosigned.

"Well it sounds good ... but me and Jerry will be at his dad's house this week," Jessica retorted, simultaneously getting inside her gold Altima. "Nice day, see you two love birds tomorrow," Jessica waved then shut the door while starting her Altima. It was evident that she was trying to get home and get the drudging day of work off of her. Sandra wished that she could do the same, but she had to report to another eight-hour shift job in an hour.

"Well I better get going ... call me, Will," Sandra said then strutted off to her pearl white Toyota.

"Love you too, babe," Willie retorted then got into his .745.

He watched Sandra leave in his rearview mirror, started his car, and turned down the blasting heavy metal by his favorite group, Seven Dust. Willie then pulled out of the parking lot and hopped behind Sandra while thinking about how he was only hours away from destroying their Florida Governor Jimmy McCarthy's race for the White House.

He wasn't fit to be our damn president. *The fucker is a big manipulator, and deserves to be in jail for what he's done,* Willie thought vengefully.

An hour later, Willie had come to the end of writing his scandalous secret on his computer. Willie leaned back in his comfy chair and stretched his arms behind his head. He then extended his arms and cracked his knuckles.

"Okay, let's print and save this beautiful masterpiece —"
Click! Clack!

"What the fuck!" Willie shouted as he jumped out of his seat after hearing the distinctive sound of a gun being cocked back. When he saw the beautiful light-skinned chick aiming a gun at him, Willie shit his pants. Ayesha loved the frightened ones.

"So, what is your beautiful masterpiece?" Ayesha asked, while starting at the computer screen displaying a lengthy report on his email.

"Who the hell are you, lady?!" Willie shouted.

"My name is, Murderlicious, Willie —"

"How the hell do you know me?" Willie asked as he balled up both of his large fists.

Cracker, I wish you would, Ayesha thought sensing that Willie was contemplating on pouncing upon her. If he did then, Ayesha had a trick or two for him.

"So, tell me Willie what is it that you're calling a masterpiece can —"

Before Ayesha could say another word Willie charged her. With nimble reaction, Ayesha side-stepped Willie and kicked out his legs from behind with a swift kick to the back of his knees. When Willie went down, Ayesha smashed him in the back of his head with the butt of her .9mm and sent him face down to the plush white carpet, unconscious.

"I love it when you motherfuckas try to play yourself," Ayesha said then took a seat in Willie's plush chair. Ayesha swayed in the chair from side to side, until her interest dwelled on Willie's scandal report.

What the fuck is this creep up to? Ayesha thought as she read the report about Governor Jimmy McCarthy; a man she was preparing to vote for.

"To all Americans who have a right to know of the people who think they're fit to be our president. Well, for months we've been trying to figure out who's a better presidential candidate out of Ben Scott and Jimmy McCarthy. Two oil and water Governors with two things in common. They're both dirty manipulators that don't give an ounce of care about America. Well, for a week I've been planning to release some truthful information about McCarthy. He's a part of a lethal CIA special ops that goes around killing government supporters and people who hold a serious threat to him ... yes, it is true and I can prove it.

In 1979, Mr. McCarthy was a part of the CIA, and responsible for a special ops team that killed other Americans. Do we want a man who'd killed other Americans in cold blood as our President –

"Man, I'mma get me a copy," Ayesha said then looked back at Willie who was coming back to the world.

Shit! Ayesha thought wanting to continue to read the report, that was very lengthy. But she refused to get caught up further. She had a job to, do and it was time for Willie's termination.

I wonder how the hell do he knows all this shit, Ayesha thought as she turned around and saw that Willie was no longer on the floor.

What the –

Before she could get her thought situated, Willie leaped out from behind the chair and wrapped his massive hands around Ayesha's throat, causing her to drop her weapon.

"Bitch, who are you!" Willie exclaimed as he throttled Ayesha with all of his might. Ayesha's face turned purple as her oxygen was being cutoff. Willie was so caught up in taking Ayesha out that he was open for an attack. Ayesha took her last hope, drilled her knee into Willie's jawline, and knocked his lights out again. As his body collapsed on her, she pushed his 210 pounds to the carpet. Ayesha touched her neck and immediately felt a sting from the bloody scratches he left on her neck from digging his nails into her.

Fuck! Ayesha thought, realizing that Willie had her DNA on him.

She bent down, grabbed her .9mm off the floor, and aimed at Willie's torso.

Psst! Psst! Psst! Psst! Psst! – after hitting Willie five times, his breathing had come to an end. Though he was now dead, Ayesha still had work to do.

Ayesha walked into Willie's small apartment kitchen and removed a butcher's knife from a knife holder. She then looked around until she found a plastic Ziploc bag.

"This'll do just fine!" she said, satisfied, then returned back to the bedroom. Ayesha knelt down next to Willie and grabbed his hand. She looked closely at his fingernails and found what she was looking for; her blood and skin from her neck underneath Willie's nails. One by one, Ayesha chopped both hands off of Willie, then placed them inside of the Ziploc bag. She then pulled from her pocket a matte crimson lipstick and painted Willie's lips a crimson red, like her superiors had ordered her to do.

"Now you're part of the clan, Willie," Ayesha said, then began deleting the report on his computer, after printing out a copy for herself.

Ayesha then walked into Willie's kitchen again and found a frying pot on the stove, already filled with frying grease. Ayesha turned the eye on, and waited for the grease to get hot. When she heard the popping of the grease, Ayesha dropped Willie's two hands inside the fryer and listened to it sizzle. The smell of the flesh being fried was horrible, but Ayesha had to do what she had to do. Ayesha left the apartment with no doubt that her DNA was gone.

Ayesha returned back to her hotel room and took a soothing hot shower, then applied antibiotic cream to her neck. It was as she was standing in front of the bathroom mirror when her Verizon flip phone chimed. She picked up the phone from off the sink and answered.

"Hello?"

"Please enter your code name." – *Beep!*

Ayesha quickly entered – Murderlicious.

"Thank you, please wait for your representative," the automated voice said, then put Ayesha on hold with Jazz music playing in the background. It was a moment before Ayesha heard the familiar voice of her representative.

"Murderlicious?" he asked for assurance.

"Yes, it is me," Ayesha retorted,

"Quickly leave the city, do not stop nowhere else or speak to no one, your target has been discovered, and a witness has placed a woman of your description leaving the apartment."

What the fuck! Ayesha thought.

"But how, I was extremely careful —"

"It happens sometime, the good news is that you're nowhere near the scene now ... good job, Murderlicious. Now please return to Philadelphia," Ayesha's representative said then hung up the phone.

Damnit! Ayesha thought, then in a hastened manner gathered all of her belongings, and made an exit from the hotel.

* * *

WILLIE SPRUCE'S murder was one of the murders that just couldn't go under the radar or be considered a common murder in a small town. He was, in fact, in the statistics of everyone else who was assassinated in connection of supporting either candidate of the Presidential race for the White House. Willie Spruce was due to report to a local radio station after he exposed the scandalous report about Governor McCarthy. The breaking news quickly spread across the Country, and had people worried who lived next to Willie Spruce. Being that he was considered a link to what was called "Government Assassins," the FBI was stepping in to muscle the case from the locals.

Director of FBI Nick Young wasted no time assigning Agents Spencer and Flynn to the case. Together, both agents boarded a special military jet and arrived in Stuart, Florida, precisely in three hours. When the duo arrived at the crime scene shortly after midnight, the crime scene was still active with local CSI everywhere, searching for some piece of evidence. Spencer and Flynn presented their credentials to two homicide detectives and instantly earned a bad rapport.

"FBI Special Agent Jackie Flynn, and this is my partner Special Agent Steven Spencer. I'm sure you guys were expecting us," Agent Flynn said to the two male detectives.

Their names were Johnson and Smith, and were both veteran homicide detectives. Johnson was a short, stubby pot belly white man in his fifties, opposed to his partner of twelve years, who was also a white, tall lean man twelve years younger than Johnson. With feigned gentleness, Detective Johnson stuck out his hand and shook Flynn's hand gently.

"Acourse we were expecting you guys, mind if we take a walk so that I can brief you two," Johnson said then turned on his heels and led the duo back into the apartment complex.

"Neighbor smells smoke as she walks out of her apartment. She hears the smoke alarms and tries the door finding it open ..." Johnson explained to Spencer and Flynn as they all strutted up the stairs to Willie Spruce's landing.

"When she peeks her head in, she sees the fire torching the stove area. She sees no Mr. Spruce and run to the only room in the apartment, where she found Mr. Spruce's body in a very gruesome state," Johnson explained as he entered Willie's apartment. Spencer and Flynn immediately took notice of the partially burnt kitchen.

"Fire rescue responded before the fire could destroy the place," Detective Smith added,

"What did the neighbor say about the strange woman she saw leave prior to discovering the fire?" Agent Spencer asked while looking around the place still swarming with CSI veterans.

"She never had seen the lady ever at Spruce's place before. And described her as a beautiful African American ..." Johnson replied,

"Have everyone who'd known that Mr. Spruce was about to release a scandalous statement against the governor been questioned?" Agent Flynn asked as the foursome moved on into the bedroom, where the outline of Willie's body as sprayed on the plush carpet.

"Everyone, except our local radio station —"

"We're seizing his computers for a start. Anything that you've seen that strikes you guys as uncommon?" Flynn asked while looking around the room.

"Hell unless Mr. Spruce cross dress, I find it weird that he had lipstick on his lips —"

"Lipstick, why the hell is that sounding off an alarm in my head?" Spencer stated.

"Because, it's similar to what a serial killer is doing —"

"In the Philadelphia area," Spencer finished.

"Could this be connected, and from the same killer?" Spencer asked Flynn who was beating her mind for an understanding.

"Not unless this is a copycat killing." Flynn retorted.

"Where's Spruce's body at?" Spencer asked Johnson.

"And we need to speak with someone from Philadelphia ... I got a feeling in my gut that something bigger than what we're expecting is going on," said Agent Flynn.

"Johnson, it's nice of you and your partner to inform us of these facts —"

"It's a pleasure working with you two," said Smith.

"The same goes for us, but now we need you guys to leave the scene. The FBI has officially taken over," Flynn said.

Cunt! Smith thought. He hated the FBI and their I run the world attitude. *Flattered bitches!*

"You fuckers think that you run the world, fuck you —"

"Smith! We will not display inappropriate conduct to our fella officials," Johnson said to his partner between clenched teeth. He too hated the FBI, but knew that to act unprofessionally would only prove that they were indeed unfit for their experience.

"Agent Flynn and Spencer, we would with no problem remove our men to let you guys start your investigation. Once again, it's a pleasure to work with you guys as well as meet the two of you. Now would you please excuse us, our job is done here," said Johnson then beckoned for Smith to follow him as he walked off.

Spencer and Flynn watched the two detectives leave and soon saw the swarm of CSI veterans depart in sections also. On both agents' minds were a puzzle that was missing a couple pieces. Neither of them had any clue of the headache to come and that the homicide was unrelated to what they would soon discover, but was done by the same killer. Nor did they know that their victim's hands were chopped off and fried. It was the information that the detectives left out on the purpose, and what they would only learn later, when it was time for them to see Willie Spruces' body.

* * *

GETTING a call from the Chief in the middle of the night could be nothing other than urgent. Cranmer was in his study of his home reviewing Eastwood's case when his cellphone chimed in. The Chief told him precisely to pack a sleep over bag and meet Lindsey at the airport to board an emergency flight to Florida. Cranmer then called Lindsey, who advised him that the sudden emergency was pertinent to their investigation. And could be a break to solve the recent murders. There was nothing more that Cranmer wanted, but to solve Eastwood's murder for the sake of his family.

Forty-five minutes later Cranmer met Lindsey in the lobby of the airport with a fresh cup of steaming coffee for Cranmer.

"Thought you'll need it until the Sunshine State is able to warm us both," Lindsey said as she handed Cranmer his coffee. It was the beginning of fall and yet it felt like winter.

"Thanks, Christina ... when are we scheduled to leave?"

"In about thirty minutes," Lindsey said then blew some steam off of her coffee.

"What are the details?" Cranmer asked as he sat down in the seat next to Lindsey.

"The victim was branded, and he doesn't appear to be a cross dresser," Lindsey informed Cranmer.

"Really?"

"That's exactly what I told Chief," Lindsey retorted.

"I don't like the sound of this one, Lindsey."

"That I do agree with ... this shit is crazy."

CHAPTER 19

Out of nowhere, Ayesha was hit with a wave of depression thinking about her father. Sitting on her sofa watching the news channel, Ayesha felt so alone despite her contentedness with Young Zoe. He was definitely a new chapter in her life, but no happiness in the world could assuage the pain that still dwelled within her of losing her father. Ayesha stood from the sofa and walked into the kitchen where her father's file sat on the kitchen table. She sat down and rubbed her temples to relieve the stress a little to no avail. Ayesha opened the file and stared at the younger mugshot of her father and saw a reflection of herself. She reflected back on the conversation she had with the detective before she'd killed him. *The Pimptress tried to bring my father down, and he was taking care of her ass,* Ayesha thought then flipped to where she'd left off last in the file.

If she played that close and betrayed him, then how close was the killer? And if the DC cats were for my dad, then who were his primary enemies? Ayesha wanted to know. She then began to read more interrogation reports. The more she read, the intensity of her anger increased, and after an hour of reading caused her to dress into an all-black attire; and vanish off into the night.

* * *

YOUNG ZOE HATED he feeling of someone going over his head. When he learned of the North Philly cats that were slain on 12th and Huntingdon, he knew beyond a doubt that Boss was behind the slaying. Though he referred it as advice not to respond to two of his soldiers' deaths, Young Zoe meant it as an order. The news was already placing his name next to violence, and that's heat that he didn't want on his name. Young Zoe was a get money nigga who handle his dirt furtively. The Youngin' inside of him died ten years ago for a reason. He was where he was today, because he started thinking like a boss would think.

He'd placed Boss on the throne of South Philly to control his drug operation, while he pursued his career in rap. Now Young Zoe was second thinking, wondering did he make a mistake making the DC cat boss of the underworld. Young Zoe wasn't afraid of Boss to not confront him about going over his head. He would see to it that Boss heard his thoughts of going against his better judgement. He knew that Boss at times could be hardheaded, but he still had a superior to think about his dirt reflecting on. Young Zoe watched the highway chase his tour bus and thought about Ayesha from time to time. He hadn't told Bos about him and Ayesha's fling, because he knew that Boss wasn't feeling it. But Young Zoe didn't give a fuck about what Boss thought of who he chose to fuck with. He was the boss and had to answer to no nigga. Young Zoe picked up his iPhone and called Ayesha's phone again, and like the last three times reaching her, it was to no avail.

I wonder where the hell is she at ... probably sleep, Young Zoe thought then became attentive to the news in Philadelphia. For the umpteen time, they were displaying the murder scene that occurred the night he'd performed in Tampa, Florida. In spite of knowing where he was on the night of the murders. The hip hop gossip still managed to declare that Young Zoe could've sent the hit, like he'd sent the hit to have Breezy killed. The news then reported that the lipstick serial killer was now reaching out to victims in Florida.

"Damn, what creep could be doing that shit?" Young Zoe exclaimed to Bone, who was sitting in the passenger seat.

"Someone who got a thang for lipstick, and had beef for Raekon," Bone said.

Young Zoe's thoughts instantly went back to the day Boss showed him photos of Raekon macking with Ayesha, an hour before his death. Young Zoe made a mental note to ask Ayesha what she had going on with Raekon. He never ran across the possible thought that Ayesha could be the killer. Had he seen the unidentified woman in the surveillance. Young Zoe would have had positively identified Ayesha as the woman. In spite of her disguise, her curvaceous body, walk, and everything about her was unique. But he was still far from knowing the woman he was falling for, and had taken her father from.

Lately, the guilt of killing Tommy Gun had been eating at his conscience. And it was always when he was in Ayesha's presence. He couldn't believe that the little girl he'd left hugging her lifeless father had turned into a beautiful woman. Now he was lovesick, because he couldn't reach that beautiful woman.

Damn! Where the hell is she at? Young Zoe thought as he tried Ayesha's number again, to no avail getting in contact with her.

"Yo' Dee, head over to "Paradise Island," change of plans," Young Zoe said to his driver.

"I got you, boss man," Dee retorted, then navigated towards Ayesha's residence.

Don't worry baby, daddi coming to wake you up, Young Zoe thought, not knowing what to expect upon his arrival because he barely knew the woman he was yearning for.

"Damn nigga, shorty eye ballin' the shit out of you," Bo said to Lil' Kenny who was sitting at the bar in the strip club on 120th and Texas. The joint was owned by an old-school cat named Rodney, and ran by Li'l Kenny, who as well was a lieutenant for Boss in his drug operation. The badass chick seemed to be interested in Li'l Kenny who was feeling himself, after copulating with Bianca's finest piece of worth, Rosa. He'd been after Rosa for some time now and had finally convinced her to bow down to his money. Rosa hated L'il Kenny and

Bo for killing her stepbrother who was indebted the Li'l Kenny and refused to pay up. In spite of her ill will towards him, she yields to Li'l Kenny's money. When he threatens to make a complaint to her boss, Rosa feared what Bianca would do to her like all of her prostitutes and conceded. Now a badass red skinned bitch, who Li'l Kenny and Bo have never seen, was sweating him.

"Bra, she looks like she by herself in this bitch, go get that bitch before I —"

Before Bo could finish boosting his boy on, Li'l Kenny strutted off heading for the chick.

Bo sat back at the bar and watched the chick beckon Li'l Kenny to follow her to a back booth, he thought then took a sip from his cup of Hennessey. He then looked at the stripper named "Pink Pussy" work the pole artistically. Bo was fucked up 'bout Pink Pussy who was a petite five-foot-three-inch,125-pound biracial chick, who was Rodney's best stripper. The ballers and players instantly made it rain twenty-dollar bills, and no less.

* * *

Li'l Kenny followed the badass chick to the back-room booth and sat down opposite of her. She wasn't wearing nothing flashy and only in an all-black attire. Her curves were still accentuating delicately in her leather, tight fitting pants. Her bosom was peeping from behind her leather fur jacket, she had partially, open revealing cleavage.

"What's up Ma?!" Li'l Kenny spoke.

"You tell me, Li'l Kenny!" Ayesha retorted. 'Li'l Kenny became alarmed when he heard the stranger mention him by his name.

"Do we know each other?!" Li'l Kenny asked as he tried to recall seeing Ayesha at some other place and time before. He was only busting his balls trying to place her anywhere.

"You don't know me, but I know you and I want to get out of here. Just me and you," Ayesha seductively while placing her boot between Li'l Kenny's legs.

Li'l Kenny smiled at Ayesha then said, "Oh yeah?"

"Yes, Li'l Kenny, come and let Keke make your night a night to remember!" Ayesha said, then stood up and walked off.

Li'l Kenny looked at her apple shape ass, and gave his dick a squeeze that was slowly arising.

"I gotta get this bitch." Li'l Kenny said then stood and followed Ayesha who he didn't know at all. When he looked over at the bar he saw that Bo was giving him the thumbs up. With that gesture, Li'l Kenny knew that nothing pretty as Ayesha could go wrong for him. She wanted to fuck, and Li'l Kenny was all for it.

When Li'l Kenny stepped outside he looked around for Ayesha. He looked to his left and didn't see her, but when he looked right he saw her walking down the ave on the sidewalk. *Where the hell is she heading at?* Li'l Kenny thought then took off after Ayesha. Ayesha turned down an alley, and it took Li'l Kenny a couple seconds to catch up. When he bent the corner, he saw Ayesha leaning against the wall with her foot copped up on the wall.

"Damn baby girl –" Before Li'l Kenny could finish speaking, Ayesha chopped him in his neck. Li'l Kenny grabbed his throat and tried breathing for fresh air.

"Bitch!" he managed to let come out. Ayesha laughed then kicked his legs from under him. Li'l Kenny felled on his back while still holding his throat. Ayesha then climbed on top of Li'l Kenny and shoved her .9mm underneath his nuts.

"Tell me, Li'l Kenny, ten years ago you worked for Tommy Gun. Who killed my father?"

"Tommy Gun ... he's your father, girl 'em down with yo daddy." Li'l Kenny said finally getting back to normal. But with a gun shoved to his nuts anything could go wrong. Looking at Ayesha Li'l Kenny could now see the resemblance of Tommy Gun in Ayesha. But he was perplexed, because Tommy Gun's daughter name wasn't Keke.

"Tommy Gun never told us he had a daughter named Keke."

"'Em not asking you that Li'l Kenny. You and yo' boy Bo was the last watch for my daddy. Who killed him?" Ayesha asked with such a cold look in her eyes.

"Keke, we don't know who killed Tommy Gun ... what can I tell you?"

"So, you get down with the D.C niggas are they responsible?" Ayesha asked then placed the gun to the side of Li'l Kenny's temple.

"Hell no, them DC niggas loved your daddy, honestly I don't know —"

Psst! Psst! Psst!

Before Li'l Kenny could finish what seemed to be everyone's answer. Ayesha pulled the trigger sending three slugs into Li'l Kenny's skull. She then retrieved her matte lipstick, and applied a coat to his lips as blood trickled out the side of his mouth.

"Don't worry sexy I'll get to the truth —" Ayesha turned around abruptly and squeezed off rapid shots hitting a homeless man. She had no clue of whom it was, the last thing she would do was take a chance with anybody. She was startled and felt no empathy for the homeless man. Ayesha got up off of Li'l Kenny and walked over to the lifeless homeless man. Ayesha knelt down and also applied lipstick to his lips.

"One time for our special guest," Ayesha said as she finished painting the homeless man lips. Ayesha then fled the area without further conflict.

Feeling a little better after releasing her anger Ayesha headed back home to get off of the streets. Things were sure about to heat up and she didn't want to be out like a sore thumb. When she pulled up to her condo in her .745 she parked next to her Porsche. For a moment, Ayesha left the car idling as she laid back in her seat and rubbed her temples. She then grabbed her iPhone off of the car charger and booted it up. After entering her password digits, she saw the persistent missed calls from Young Zoe.

"Damnit, he probably —"

"What the funk!" Ayesha shouted startled from the raps at her window. Ayesha had her .9mm out in a flash aiming at the surprised guest.

"Damn boo, you packing with speed huh?" Young Zoe said as he held his hands in the air in surrender.

"Oh shit …" Ayesha said as she put the gun back into her holster on the inside of her leather jacket.

"'Em sorry baby" she retorted then opened the door, and jumped into Young Zoe's arms. Ayesha kissed Young Zoe's lips then slide her tongue into his mouth as he palmed her ass. He'd startled her and she wasn't customed to the unannounced visits, but she was happy to see her man.

"It's okay baby, I'm glad you're strap and it looks like you know what you are doing with it boo," Young Zoe acknowledged.

"I know a thang or two, it's called protection … this is Philadelphia baby," Ayesha explained,

"Yeah it is baby, but you don't have to worry about nobody fuckin' wit you boo," Young Zoe said then kissed Ayesha slow and passionately.

"Thanks baby," Ayesha retorted.

"But you still never know, let's not be naïve baby."

"Acourse … I miss you girl," Young Zoe said as he backed Ayesha up against the car and began to caress her ass.

"Come home with me tonight," Young Zoe demanded Ayesha then kissed her softly again. When he began sucking on Ayesha's neck she let out a soft moan and wanted Young Zoe to take her right there in the parking lot. Her pussy was moist and hot, and definitely yearning to be touch by Young Zoe.

"Let's go … baby," Ayesha said ready to go wherever Young Zoe had in mind to take her.

* * *

SINCE ARRIVING in Florida Cranmer and Lindsey spent the entire day in the Marion County precinct down in Stuart, Florida getting acquainted with Spencer and Flynn. Who Cranmer found very intriguing working with them. After taking a look at the victim Willie Spruce and the photos from the crime scene, Cranmer was doubtless that their lipstick killer was responsible for the Florida murder. But why take a trip to Florida and target a man who the government would've killed themselves.

What was irksome to Cranmer and had him scratching his head was the mutilation of Willie's hands, and them being fried. It wasn't the killer's M.O. and had slightly created skepticism and caused Cranmer and Lindsey to consider a copycat. But something strong had prevented them to believe such a theory that the murder was done by a copycat. It was the perfection of how the lipstick was applied without any overlapping. Which meant that in all of the previous cases, the killer had experience with using lipstick. Cranmer didn't want to finalize his second thoughts of the killer being woman. He would see how long it took his partner to think commonsensical of the logical theory.

Cranmer and Lindsey had retired from the scene and precinct with FBI agents Spencer and Flynn an hour ago. As soon as dawn came, the duo would be back on their way to Philadelphia to continue their investigation in their city. The Florida case was in the hands of the FBI and when that happened, it was only assisting that could be done by the locals to accommodate the FBI. Both Cranmer and Lindsey rented out a hotel room with two separate beds and waited for dawn. They were both exhausted from flying out to Florida, walking through the scene, seeing the gruesome sight of Willie, and interrogating anyone close to the victim. They were grateful for the rest, especially Lindsey, who was out cold in the queen-size bed. Cranmer sat in a chair in a corner of the room and was doing some serious thinking, trying to find sense of the murders. But like it's been lately for him he would always come to a dead end.

What woman could take down a six-three, 210 pounds German? thought Cranmer as his phone chimed loudly causing Lindsey to stir in her sleep. Cranmer answered the phone before it woke Lindsey.

"Hello?"

"Cranmer, how's progress big guy? the Chief of Police asked.

"It's still an enigma boss … 'em tipping my belief that our suspect may be a woman —"

"No way," said the Chief.

"I felt the same way until something related to all murders stuck out."

"And what is that, Cranmer?"

"The lipstick on all victims is applied perfect with no mistakes or even a hint of a mistake," Cranmer explained as he watched Lindsey get out of bed and walk into the restroom. She was good and up now.

"That's good grounds to consider, Cranmer ... but it doesn't seal the deal with that consideration alone," said the Chief.

"Acourse it don't, but it brings us to some light in the tunnel."

"Let's determine that when we take a look at our two new victims," said the Chief.

"Are you serious, boss?" Cranmer said as he became extra alarmed. He heard the toilet in the bathroom being flushed followed by the water at the sink running.

"Son, I wouldn't kid you. Camilla is in charge right now until you two make it back into town. Two were found in an alley on 120th and Texas in South Philly. But there's something odd in this one —"

"What is it Chief?" Cranmer asked,

"One's a small-time hustler, and the other is a homeless man who'd just got released from jail days ago."

"Damnit," Cranmer cursed. "And you said Camilla is on this one?"

"She's out there now doing everything to preserve the scene for you and Lindsey. The bodies will still be there when you two arrive," Chief explained.

"Okay boss, I'll call you when we land in Philly," said Cranmer as Lindsey walked out of the bathroom and sat on the edge of the bed, rubbing her temples.

"See you guys soon," the Chief said then hung up the phone. Cranmer sighed then kicked his long legs out, and crossed his arms across his chest.

"What is it, Cranmer?" Lindsey asked already knowing when there was a new discovery at hand.

"They found two more lipstick murders in an alley on 120th and Texas. Camilla is working the scene until we arrive."

"You gotta be kidding me, Cranmer," Lindsey retorted while

looking at her partner, wishing he would concede that he was joking around. But she knew her partner well not to even play games with his job. He took his job just like she did to the heart and for the victim's sake, he gave 100% as far as his integrity and dedication.

"That's exactly what I told the Chief, and he wished that he was," Cranmer explained.

"Great, now the fucker wants to play jump around," Lindsey exclaimed then laid back on the bed frustrated.

"The killings are a day apart, we check the airlines thoroughly, Florida, and Philly," Cranmer explained,

"It's a start, big guy."

"Exactly what we need, Lindsey," said Cranmer.

"Wake me up when it's time to go?" Lindsey said then closed her eyes, trying to catch sleep that just wouldn't be found. Too much was running through her vagrant mind, and she had no clue how to stop going into overdrive.

"We have to find this killer, Cranmer, and I mean find them fast," said Lindsey.

"We will, Christina, just stay focused with me, okay?" Lindsey turned her head and looked Cranmer in his sincere eyes.

"Yes, Cranmer, I will," she promised her partner, solemnly.

"Man, this shit isn't looking good, Youngin'. How you gonna tell me 'em acting off of emotions nigga and my men fallin' dead around this bitch!" Boss exclaimed to Young Zoe.

They were in the back seat of Boss' limousine in privacy while Tank and Bone stood outside keeping each other company.

"Man Boss, check this out. Yeah, it's crazy how shit happens —"

"Nigga shit ain't happen. Our men were targeted Youngin' what the fuck you've been on lately my nigga?"

"What the fuck do you think nigga?" I been on getting money, and representing out city —"

"Yo' city nigga, 'em from DC," Boss retorted like a vicious animal.

"Oh, so you talking like that, huh?" Young Zoe questioned Boss who knew that what he said was a slap to Young Zoe's face. But he was tired of washing a nigga back who'd forgotten who he was, and was doing stupid shit like sleeping with an enemy's daughter.

Boss had seen Ayesha when Young Zoe pulled up to his condo in South Philly. When he approached Young Zoe, he didn't like how Ayesha was giving him an evil look, so he gave her one and held his tongue when wanting to check her like he'd do any other bitch. It was out of respect for Young Zoe that he didn't snake out on her. But now he was fed up with Young Zoe's too good to bust his gun attitude.

"Naw'll nigga, it's like that," Boss responded to Young Zoe, whose fist was balled up ready to pounce on Boss. Boss pulled out his Glock .40 from underneath his thigh and placed it on his lap.

"Nigga, we came in this together with a real vision. Now that you hall of fame, you full of hubris nigga, and done let forbidden pussy poison yo' mind, nigga. 'Em in a different world than you and gotta play by the rules of the game. You not Youngin' no more —"

"Nigga, I'll always be Youngin'!" Young Zoe snapped.

Boss had some nerves pulling his gun out on him like he was some pussy in the game. Boss had never disrespected Young Zoe. What Young Zoe was realizing was that Boss wasn't the same Fat Boy that he'd brainwashed and used as a pawn, and manipulated out of a career. Boss had come to his senses on that realization, and only saw one way to fix it. And it was the reason why he'd showed lieutenant was killed.

"Yeah, you'll always be Youngin' and I'll always be Fat Boy. So, with that said, 'em done being dumbass Boss complacent to a kingpin who only thinks about himself. Youngin' this my shit out here. If you want to pull yo' men back, us DC niggas don't mind. Know what I mean, son?"

"So, what you saying, nigga?" Young Zoe asked Boss with an ominous look on his face.

"'Em saying nigga, you bleed too. Ain't no more operation, the streets mines. With yo' plugs or not, we DC niggas got good connections with good product nigga."

"Nigga I made you, nigga! You can't —"

Click! Clack! Boss cocked the gun back.

"Make me, nigga," Boss said with his gun aimed in Young Zoe's face.

"Bye Youngin', I'll see you around, and by the way Fat Boy MC is back, too. Now please leave my presence before I do something I don't want to do," Boss informed Young Zoe who bridled his pride and started for the door never taking his eyes off of Boss and the muzzle of the gun.

"You right Fat Boy, you'll see me around," Young Zoe said then exited the limousine.

Young Zoe and Bone watched the limousine leave the condo complex in silence that made Bone sense something wrong.

"Is everything cool, boss man?" Bone asked as he sparked flame to a Newport cigarette.

"Yeah everything cool until we burn every DC nigga in sight," Young Zoe said to Bone then strutted off to go cozy up with his new queen, a woman who he couldn't tell his darkest secret to, if it was to save his life revealing it. Then Young Zoe would be a dead man. Young Zoe couldn't believe Boss' impudence towards him, and now understood thoroughly that all good things do come to an end.

Ayesha knew that something was troubling Young Zoe. He just wasn't the same as he was before his boy Boss pulled up to visit him. Though his performance in the bed wasn't no different, she still sensed discomfort. Laying in Young Zoe's arms in bed, she could hear his rapid heartbeat.

"Baby, are you okay?" Ayesha asked, defeating her curiosity. Young Zoe looked down at Ayesha and kissed her on her forehead.

"Baby, there aren't any problems that I can't deal with to not worry you. Baby, I'm okay," Young Zoe retorted, skeptical of his own belief.

Shit was about to turn up, because the last thing Young Zoe would do was back down from any nigga. Boss had definitely played him and had now forced his hands. With friction soon to come now, he was determined to know who side would most of his homies be on. Fat Boy, who over the years had won the loyalty of many solid niggas, including his niggas who'd migrated from DC to Philadelphia. Or the face of Philadelphia, and notorious gun slinger – Youngin'.

"Just know that I'm here for you baby, and I can handle anything a man could handle," Ayesha stated, breaking Young Zoe's thoughts. At that moment, he detected an unusual strength in Ayesha that a lot of women lacked. These days it was portrayal of a Ride or Die Bitch!

It made him wonder about her and Raekon, and probe the matter.

"Ayesha, can I ask you a question?"

"Go ahead, baby," Ayesha said as she sat up and looked in Young Zoe's disturbed eyes.

"Word came to me that you and a cat named Raekon Adams were getting to know each other before his death. Is it true?" Young Zoe asked, searching Ayesha's eyes for any hint of evading her honesty. He had the pictures, now did he have a real bitch in front of him?

"Yeah, I know Raekon and he died the day I met him. We were supposed to meet up at the hotel. But when I got there he was already dead —"

"Damn Ma, that's crazy."

"Yeah it is; but it's life, what could anyone do about it?"

"What do you think about the lipstick serial killer, they say that's who killed him too?"

"I think that she's a bad bitch," Ayesha said with a smirk on her face so ominous looking that told Young Zoe that she had a taste for blood. *She's definitely a ride or die bitch,* Young Zoe thought as he lifted Ayesha's chin and looked into her eyes.

"Would you kill a nigga if it was to save my life?" he asked Ayesha.

"Baby, I will kill a nigga even if yo' life wasn't in harm's way. All he has to do is rub off on you the wrong way," Ayesha retorted.

"Damn you're so much like your daddy," Young Zoe said.

"And that's exactly what I will make his killer say before I kill him," Ayesha said as she looked the killer, unbeknownst to her, in his eyes. Young Zoe was lost for words. All he could do is grab a hold of Ayesha as she broke down in his arms. The tough girl had vanished and he was now seeing the hurt of a lost nine-year-old, who'd seen her father murdered in cold blood. As Ayesha cried, Young Zoe laid her back and began to make love to her.

"I got you, ma ... we in this together," Young Zoe said as he kissed Ayesha's salty tears. As he slid into her love box, Ayesha's cries fluctuated to moans of pleasure and contentedness.

"Mmm! Mmm ... Dayvon!" she purred as he stroked her slow, and she caressed the back of his head and back.

CHAPTER 20

*L*ike the Chief had promised, the two victims' bodies were still on the crime scene a little past 8 o'clock in the morning. The sun was shining bright and did a little to keep Cranmer, Lindsey, and everyone else on the crime scene warm, against the cold winds. Feeling winter in the break of fall hinted a cold damn winter on its way. Cranmer and Lindsey met with Camilla who was sitting in her SUV trying to keep warm with a cup of coffee, and food from McDonald's. Camilla stepped out of the SUV with her coffee in hand, and a skully cap over her head and ears.

"Glad that you two are here, the undertaker is on his way to get the bodies."

"I'm sure it's been hell for you Camilla," Lindsey expressed with her hands inside her thick jacket that had "PPD" stamped on the back in white letters. There were a lot of other "Philadelphia Police Department" officers as well wearing their issued jackets. Lindsey had had her jacket since the beginning of her career as a police, as well as Cranmer.

"So, what do we have?" Cranmer asked as the trio walked towards the alley on 120th and Texas.

"Kenny James Jr. aka Li'l Kenny, a small-time hustler since the late kingpin Tommy Gun Jordan. Witnesses says he was last seen leaving the strip joint he co-owns – with an unidentified woman."

"So were back to an unidentified woman," Cranmer said as he stepped over the yellow crime scene tape at the mouth of the alley and immediately saw the two bodies underneath white shrouds.

"No surveillance, so we have no tapes of them to figure out who is this woman," Camilla informed Cranmer and Lindsey as Cranmer knelt down and pulled the shroud back. When he saw the victim Kenny James Jr. he knew exactly who he was.

"A long time ago, I told this fella to get out of the streets while he had a chance ... he was working for Tommy Gun," Cranmer said.

"And was his watch, him, and his boy Bo on the night Tommy Gun and Quavis was killed," Camilla added.

It was her and Eastwood's case until the FBI swept in and took over. Cranmer looked at Li'l Kenny's lips and saw what he was looking for. The flawless lipstick that only a person with an experience could do. *Like a woman,* Cranmer considered.

"The homeless man ... do he has lipstick on him, too?" Cranmer asked while staring at Li'l Kenny's lips.

"Yeah, he's wearing some crimson too," Camilla answered.

Cranmer stood and shook his head. He didn't need to see the homeless man to determine his final conclusion. There was no doubt in his mind that the killer was a woman. A woman with unusual capabilities of a woman's strength. Whoever she was, she knew what she was doing. But he still had no motive of why she was doing it.

"Do you still believe these aren't a woman's capabilities?" Cranmer asked Lindsey with a smile on his face. Camilla had been around long enough to notice that one detective had out smarted the other.

* * *

BOSS WAS serious about cutting Young Zoe off and knew what was to come after pulling his gun on Young Zoe. He knew that Young Zoe wasn't a pussy by a long shot. But what was done and said was done. Boss had summoned all his Sergeants and soldiers he'd ranked from the streets to meet at his mansion. Every man attending the rendezvous was from the DC area. Something that Young Zoe was too caught up in himself to notice that his right-hand had been preparing to break up for years. Amongst him, out of twenty niggas in his back yard under a tent, were a lot who had respect for Young Zoe. But when it came to choosing sides, going against Boss would be considered Cardinal, and surely put their family members back home in DC at risk. It was known throughout the sister state's how Fat Boy got down when a nigga was on the other side of the field.

"Everyone sitting here is here because we all came from the same woods," Boss said to the men sitting at the long wooden table attentive to what he was saying.

Boss stood up from his seat and adjusted his vest to his cream Versace tailored suit. In his mouth, he had a smoking cigar.

"When one of us is crossed, it don't matter when it is …" Boss said then removed the cigar from his mouth, simultaneously searching the faces of the men he'd given a chance to individually when they came running from DC after hearing Boss' name regulate to Philadelphia area. Each one came looking for a job with a pathetic story, and Boss with open arms accepted, each one out of love that they had the heart; to ask another man for help.

"We handle they ass and don't stop until they drop," Boss retorted, then took a pull from the cigar simultaneously exhaling the smoke.

"Young Zoe, who we know as Youngin' … that nigga no longer our friend. He's our enemy, and any nigga standing up for him, and with him," Boss said as he walked up to Taz and Mane sitting at the table sipping on a bottle of Remy Martin.

"Taz and Mane, I elect you two niggas as my head enforcers. From this day on, DC taking the mothership home, and populate this shit with more of DC's finest. That nigga Youngin' is a dead man walking. Who feel me in this bitch?" Boss asked then got an air full of drinks, niggas raised above their head as an assent.

"That's what 'em talking 'bout, now that's DC love," Boss said with a smile on his face.

The good deeds does pay off I see, Boss thought as he stared at all the support he had. Boss knew that things were only 'bout to get more real in the streets beefing with Young Zoe. But he also knew how to defeat Young Zoe, being that he knew him better than anyone in the rendezvous.

Boss knew that he had to watch every move he took meticulously. And to be on the lookout for a snake, trying to play two sides. He hated the fact that Li'l Kenny was killed, and that he wasn't from the DC area like Bo. Because though Bo showed no signs of disloyalty, he still had to get rid of him. Boss walked along the table and pulled out his Glock .45 from the center of his back. When he made it to Bo he placed his gun to the back of Bo's head and pulled the trigger. The men in his vicinity tried jumping out of the way to avoid the blood splatter, to no avail.

"This is how serious it is," Boss said to his men who all understood what didn't need to be explained.

"Buckhead, get rid of this nigga, toss him behind his joint on 22nd and Compus," Boss demanded his clean up man, who carried an experienced team of niggas who would turn a crime scene immaculate.

"I got you, boss man," Buckhead retorted then got on the phone with his crew.

"The rest of you guys, this meeting is over, and war have just begun," Boss said, then left the men who began to make their own departure from Boss' mansion.

* * *

AYESHA HAD SPENT the entire morning with Young Zoe at his studio watching him put down a new track called "Snake Nigga." It was a track where he had a chance to release so much anger, and talk directly to his newest enemy – Boss. At noon, the couple took a stroll through the mall and bought each other gifts from the jewelry department. The couple stepped out with scintillating jewels and felt like Jay and Beyoncé.

Pulling up to her condo at dusk, Ayesha didn't want her day to end with Young Zoe, and neither did he. But he had things that were important to do. And people to see that were as well important. Ayesha understood, and didn't want to seem like the stuck-up type who didn't allow their man breathing room like the common insecure bitch who had trust issues.

"So, I guess I'll hear from you later, baby," Ayesha said as she turned around in her seat facing Young Zoe.

"Don't make it sound so sad, boo," Young Zoe said then kissed Ayesha on her lips. Ayesha intensified the passionate kiss, sliding her tongue inside his mouth. The duo kissed for every bit of a minute, before they pulled away from each other.

"Call me if you need me, Dayvon."

"I will beautiful," Young Zoe said as Ayesha stepped out of the back seat of the limousine.

"Call me," Ayesha said then blew Young Zoe a kiss before she closed the door. Young Zoe watched Ayesha sashay into her condo safely before he ordered Mac to pull off. His first stop was to his personal barber for a fresh haircut.

When Ayesha stuck her key into the door she noticed, a yellow card stuck between her door. She grabbed the card and read it Call me, Brandon … Daddi in town. Ayesha sucked her teeth then entered the condo. When she stepped inside she realized how good it felt to be home. She could never get tired of having her own place. *But what if Young Zoe wanted her to move in with him would it be a different story?* Ayesha smiled at the thought and walked upstairs.

Once in her room, she pulled out her Verizon track phone from her purse and saw that no calls had been missed. Ayesha then plopped down on her bed and smiled as she began to already miss Young Zoe. As she laid there pensively thinking about her and Young Zoe, she heard someone knocking at her front door. Ayesha sucked her teeth then went to see whom it was at her door. When she looked through the peephole her heart beat accelerated.

What the fuck is he doing here?! Ayesha thought as she stared at the white man in a black suit and dark shades on his eyes. It was the same man from the mall who she'd caught trailing her. Ayesha opened the door and instinctively looked around for more company. But saw that the man was alone.

"What is it now," Ayesha asked standing akimbo.

The man dug in his pockets to his slacks and came out with another Verizon flip track phone.

"Get rid of your old phone, and be available in the next hour," the man said as he handed Ayesha her new phone.

"Thanks," Ayesha said then watched the man strut away.

"These top secret – Oh shit! Willie's report was right," Ayesha said then closed the door and dashed to the kitchen. Ayesha sat down at the table and read Willie Spruce's report that never made it to the world. *Because the CIA had killed him*, Ayesha realized.

CHAPTER 21

ONE MONTH LATER:

*T*he streets in Philadelphia had transformed into baby Pakistan with an increase in the murder rate. War was coming from all ends against Boss, who was not only at war with Young Zoe and his men, but North Philly. Who were still feeling the loss of Breezy. The beef between Boss and Young Zoe was out in the streets like a new mixtape, something that Bianca found peculiar, being that the two were once like brothers. She didn't have the merits of their fall out, she like everyone else was only seeing the aftermath of whatever caused either men to explode.

Bianca was hoping that the two once close friends killed each other. And the new bitch that Young Zoe was flaunting around proclaiming to be his woman, Bianca disliked her the first time she saw her. It was a shocking to everyone that this woman was the daughter of late legendary Tommy Gun. Her mother Ariel couldn't believe it herself until she saw Ayesha T. Jordan on TV supporting her rapper boyfriend at a concert in New York City. It was Young Zoe's fault that Bianca couldn't hang on Breezy's arm and share the fame with him. And she would make Young Zoe and Boss pay for taking her man away from her. The beef between Young Zoe and Boss was affecting her in many ways. In the last two weeks, Bianca had lost five of her prostitutes by stray bullets during drive by shootings. She was fortunate that none of them were her power house prostitutes, but it still was a loss in her eyes. She couldn't help but think of how to get her enemies that were at each other's throats out of her way.

When the limousine came to a complete stop, Bianca snapped out of her thoughts, and saw that she was at the airport where she was scheduled to board a flight to Florida to be with Danny, who had a beach house on South Beach down in Miami.

Bianca needed the vacation and felt that a new scenery for a change momentarily was good enough. Her bodyguard Al stepped out of the limo and opened the back door. Bianca stepped out and shield her eyes from the ardent sun shining down from heaven. It wasn't cold like the weather had been for the last two days. It was comfortable at 72° and stagnate winds! Bianca felt for a moment that she was already in Miami.

"Feels good out here, Al," Bianca expressed while Al carried her luggage for her.

"Yeah until midnight, if counting on the weather man is reliable," Al retorted who'd heard the weather man predict another cold front, that would stay until Christmas, and they were only in November; five days away from electing a new president.

"'Em sure we'll be alright, Al," Bianca said, as they walked inside the airport.

"Bianca Williams!" Bianca heard a woman from behind her call out her name.

Who the fuck is calling me? Bianca thought as she turned around with Al and saw two detectives, one of them who she knew as Camilla.

"Sorry to interrupt your plans, but the time has come —"

"What the fuck you talking 'bout, bitch?!" Bianca barked.

"Bianca Williams, you're under arrest ..." Camilla said as she retrieved her handcuffs and grab Bianca by her wrist, then placed her hands behind her back.

"For a number of charges, number one murder, and number two, well you already know. And by the way, all of your prostitutes are singing yo' name like Beyoncé," Camilla said in Bianca's ear.

"Well, let 'em sing it's a free country. Al, call my lawyer, and let him know what's going on," Bianca said as she was being hauled away.

Bianca couldn't believe what was occurring to her. In spite of the reality Bianca did her best to remain calm and show no fear. She'd never been incarcerated in her life, but would make it appear as if she'd being doing time her whole life. As Bianca was being escorted out the front entrance of the airport. The news cameras and multiple reporters shoved mics in her face.

"Bianca Williams, is it true that you're the Pimptress of Philadelphia?!"

"No comment," Bianca retorted as Camilla's partner jostled through the crowd of reporters helping Bianca to the back seat of an unmarked SUV.

"Bianca Williams, will you post bail?!"

"Are you innocent, Bianca?!"

The questions continued as the SUV pulled off hauling Bianca to the Philadelphia precinct.

* * *

YOUNG ZOE COULDN'T BELIEVE that the Pimptress had just been arrested. He thought that girl was on her shit. *Apparently, she went wrong somewhere,* Young Zoe thought, then began to think about Ariel, and what she was probably going through at the moment. Bianca was her bread and water, and had kept what she built alive.

"Damn I gotta go check up on Ariel and see that Bianca get the top-notch attorney," Young Zoe thought as he sat on his plush leather sofa in his living room watching the news channel.

He was laying low at his low-key condo on the outskirts of Philadelphia. No one knew of his location, but Bone, Mac and Ayesha, who was handling a business deal for her job in New Jersey, and who he hadn't seen in two days. He was yearning for her and couldn't wait to see her later on tonight like she'd promised. Since going public with their relationship, bitches from all over who was famous had been trying to get him to leave Ayesha, who was considered a threat in the beauty department.

Young Zoe knew his worth and that he had a precious stone in his life. He was in love with the late legendary Tommy Guns daughter. The man he took out with the help of three. Ariel had played her part well and he saw her as a loyal woman. It was the main reason why he wouldn't sign her daughter's death certificate. Bianca wasn't cut like her mother, but she had the game down pack that she learned from Ariel. Young Zoe thought back on the night he'd killed Tommy Gun and Quavis. Ariel had called him shortly after she'd talk with Tommy Gun who was closing down his drug operation.

Every night he called Ariel and ask how was his money looking on 54th and 61st. He was closing down his drug operation and Quavis was heading to the safe house. Without her, things wouldn't have run so smoothly that night. She was part of the take down and proved over the years that she was a down bitch in her own class. Now with her own seed in the hand of the system, Young Zoe had her loyalty in question. Loyalty had no meaning and true value when going against family. *Would she trade a decade secret to save her daughter from death now?* Young Zoe thought and realized that it was something he couldn't risk. He had to check on Ariel and at least pick her mind to determine his decision; of whether he would terminate her or let her live. When Young Zoe looked back up at the TV. He saw for the umpteen time Bianca being carried away from the airport in handcuffs.

"No comment," he heard Bianca tell the reporter and realized that in spite of her fucking with his rivals.

She seriously had the traits of her mother. *And that's a good sign thus far,* Young Zoe thought. Young Zoe was broken out of his thoughts at the chiming of his iPhone on the living room glass table. He picked up the phone and checked the caller ID and saw that it was Bone, who was now his right-hand man and enforcer in the streets.

"What's up soldier?" Young Zoe answered.

"Are you seeing what's going on?"

"Yeah, the Pimptress looks like she's in a bad situation —"

"No Youngin' 'em talking about this nigga Boss and his new track that just aired live on the radio."

"That's new to me ... What he on?"

"It's deep son, too deep," Bone retorted truthfully.

"What is it called?" Young Zoe asked simultaneously downloading the music app: "SoundCloud."

"Fat Boy vs Youngin'."

"Say What?!" Young Zoe exclaimed with a stomach forming of butterflies and a heavy heart.

"That's what I said, listen what he's saying in the track, son," Bone said then hung up the phone.

Young Zoe had the app pulled up on his phone and entered the name of the artist and song – Boss: Fat Boy vs Youngin'. The song immediately popped up and already had a tremendous number of viewers; who loved the track. Young Zoe tapped play on his screen and listened to the song begin. The beat was a mean beat and grabbed a person's attention instantly.

(Insert Music Note) "If you crossed the legend who the fuck could trust ya/Told me I wasn't shit and that music wouldn't get me rich/So I picked up the stick/Now the daughter sucking yo' dick/do you forget, ski masks and four pound was the last sound/before you took the legend down/Now it's Fat Boy vs Youngin' beating yo' block down Hunt 'em down to the 12th I empty my clip/now nigga you bitch up/The same signs when you took the legend down –"

This nigga is tripping!" Young Zoe exploded, it was no doubt that the song was a hit. The context was a hint of the ugly crime they'd did ten years ago. Who couldn't read between them lines and realized what legend he was talking about. This nigga done crossed the line for real and he can't just sabotage my name. A real nigga wouldn't mention no one's past to harm them.

All Young Zoe could think about is how would Ayesha's mind register when she heard the song. What would her thoughts be even when he tells her that a nigga would say anything for attention and money? In spite of their beef, Young Zoe would've never thought that Boss would shed light of their past to the world. He could only imagine how many ol' school niggas that was around ten years ago; was solving the mystery of Tommy Guns death. Boss did everything in his power to not mention Tommy Gun's name. But it wasn't a hint that remained an enigma, it was now extremely transparent to a lot of people. This situation only showed Young Zoe clarity of what Tommy Gun had once dropped on him about picking his friends wisely.

"You have to be careful of what you build, because the aftermath of destruction is what kills you," Tommy Gun once told Young Zoe. It was at that time when Tommy Gun was warning him about a snake, not knowing that the snake was in front of him. After Tommy Gun saw Fat Boy flow on the Mic he espied improvement, and was contemplating on giving Fat Boy a chance. Young Zoe was furious though he bridled his disapproval. He saw Fat Boy as a threat to stealing his fame, and the only way to abort Tommy Gun's intentions was to kill him.

* * *

ARIEL BECAME DISTRAUGHT when she'd first learned that her daughter was arrested. The news had come to her by Al who had to catch Ariel before she collapsed to the ground at her front door. Her shrill was loud enough to wake the entire neighborhood. Not that Al was gone Ariel sat in her living room silently crying for her daughter. She'd ran through an entire two boxes of tissue. For hours, she'd been waiting for Bianca to call. The sun was an hour away from going down and Bianca still haven't called.

The news channel continued to sabotage Bianca and made her look like some cold-blooded killer and menace to society. She knew her baby wasn't an innocent soul, but labeling her as a monster was preposterous. Ariel couldn't live an honest life without Bianca who'd saved her from the drugs that help end her reign. Ariel had let the drugs kill her beauty, and the guilty conscience of conspiracy. Her participation in betraying her lover ate at her 'til this day. She believed in Karma and felt that everyone was subject to it.

Tommy Gun was good to her and had made her the forewoman of his whore's. It was when she saw that she could muscle his goldmine when she decided to help get rid of him. Now she was wondering ... was Karma taking her course. If it was she couldn't sit around and watch it destroy her only child. Ariel planned to die with the truth of Tommy Gun's death. But now she was seeing the benefit it would bring if she used it properly; without incriminating herself. She knew the laws of being a rat, but she would do anything to save Bianca. To lose Bianca meant to lose herself. She couldn't let that happen. Ariel just hoped that Fat Boy and Youngin' didn't kill each other before she could trade her story.

Ariel couldn't believe that Young Zoe had the audacity to be dating the man's daughter. When he was the one who killed her father. Niggas could be so cold, and I know that I have no room to speak. But that is some cold shit – Ariel thoughts we're interrupted when knocks appeared at her front door. *Who the hell is this?* Ariel thought as she wiped her face with used tissue then strutted over to the front door. When Ariel checked her peephole, she saw that the visitor was Bianca's head bitch, Rosa. Ariel opened the door and smiled tentatively.

"Hi, Rosa 'em sure you've heard," Ariel said sadly with her arms folded and her hand under her armpits. When she looked in Rosa's eyes Rosa averted eyes caused her to sense something amiss. Rosa was trembling badly and it caused Ariel to ask her.

"Rosa, are you okay?"

"Yes, can I come in?" Rosa replied in a shaken voice. Ariel at first was hesitant not wanting to trust Rosa in her home with the way she was acting. But then she thought *Maybe she's taking the news bad as she did. We all need someone to support us in time like this.* With her mind decided Ariel stepped aside and walked back into the living room as Rosa stepped inside. Ariel grabbed the remote control and sat back in her spot on the sofa; sitting Indian style. When Ariel looked over at Rosa her heart dropped and began to accelerate in fear. She now understood why Rosa had been acting weird. She was being held at gun point by a familiar face woman.

"Sit down next to her bitch and stay quiet … you," Ayesha said to Ariel while pointing the gun at her and Rosa doing as she was told. "Cut the TV off now," Ayesha ordered Ariel.

Taking a closer look, Ariel had solved the resemblance, and familiarity of the armed woman in her home. *Karma in the worst way,* Ariel thought as she turned the TV off. *She looks so much like her father,* Ariel espied.

"Nice to meet you, Ariel, 'em so sorry that Bianca can't join us," Ayesha said as she took a seat in the plush La-Z-Boy.

"But it's okay, that's why I found Rosa to take her place in this important meeting," Ayesha said then looked at both frighten women impassively.

"You look so much like your father Ayesha, we're not your enemies," Ariel said in a shaky voice.

"I've heard it all my life, I just wished that he could see it to Ariel."

The report from Ayesha made Ariel's heart get heavy. Rosa had no clue of the pain both women were sharing momentarily.

"He's watching down from heaven Ayesha —"

"Don't give me that bullshit Ariel, I don't want your commiseration I want answers, Ariel. Who killed my father?!" Ayesha exclaimed in a husky voice. Ariel and Rosa saw Ayesha's pain clearly.

"Baby it's been ten years and I've been in the same place as you wondering who could be so grimy to taka a good man's life," Ariel expressed in feigned concern.

She even went to the extent of dropping her head and rubbing her temples, with a shaky hand. She had almost convinced Ayesha that she was an innocent soul, until the fact that she conspired to set her daddy up jumped out to her. Ayesha stood to her feet and walked over to Ariel. When Ariel raised her head, Ayesha slapped the shit out of Ariel with her gun causing blood to splatter onto Rosa's bosom, and cream mini dress.

"Bitch, you want to preach on grimy when you were working with the police to set my daddy up!" Ayesha exclaimed to Ariel who was crying hysterical balled up next to Rosa. Rosa herself began crying afraid that Ayesha would smack her next with the gun. Ayesha grabbed a hand full of Ariel's hair and jammed the gun underneath Ariel's chin.

"Bitch, you played my daddy when he took care of your ass, the motive was to get him out the way so that you could take full control of his prostitution operation. You was ready to sell my daddy out so you found someone to kill him am I right, Ariel?!"

"Please, Ayesha ..." Ariel sobbed, "I had nothing to do with it!" Ariel replied,

"Oh, so you had nothing to do with it, it sounds like you know something bitch!"

"Aww!!" Ariel shrilled when Ayesha smashed her in her mouth with the butt of the gun, knocking out Ariel's front grill in the process. Ayesha then reached in her pocket and came out with an all-black tube of lipstick. She was changing the game up today and going against her crimson lipstick.

"Bitch, put this on you, then on her," Ayesha said to Rosa then tossed he lipstick to Rosa.

Oh, my gosh she's the lipstick serial killer! Ariel and Rosa both put together simultaneously. The look on Rosa's face revealed to Ayesha that she'd put two and two together.

"Yeah bitch, it's me ... Murderlicious. Now do what I say before I blow yo' pretty ass all the way back to Puerto Rico bitch," Ayesha promised Rosa. Rosa didn't hesitate with trembling hands she removed her pink lipstick and applied the black lipstick.

"Now put it on this grimy ass bitch," Ayesha beckon to Rosa. Rosa reached over and removed Ariel's trembling hands from her mouth.

"Oh, my gosh!" Rosa exclaimed in her distinctive accent, when she saw Ariel's swollen lips, with blood pouring from her mouth.

"Do it, bitch!" Ayesha barked.

Rosa quickly did as she was told and applied lipstick to Ariel's swollen bloody lips. Ariel winced in pain and flinched, but continued to let Rosa decorate her swollen lips. When Rosa had finished, Ayesha turned the gun on Rosa and squeezed the trigger peeling her scalp back and sending brains all over the wall, sofa, and into Ariel's hair.

She's going to kill me! Ariel thought as she cried timorously.

"Now back to you Ariel … who killed my father, and why?" Ayesha asked as she retook her seat in the La-Z-Boy, and crossed her legs. She laid her gun on her lap and waited for Ariel to answer her.

"Ayesha, why are you hurting me? … I could have been your step-mom. That's how me and your daddy were … we were lovers, Ayesha," Ariel explained through her pain, and bloody mouth.

"Yet you still tried to slime my dad, Ariel. So, lovers wasn't on your mind then, why now?" Ayesha asked, "Or did you think your secret wouldn't get out of the bag. I read the report, and I know where you was the night of his murder. And I know that he called you before he was killed. So please don't lie to me Ariel."

Karma! Ariel thought, she badly wanted to cooperate, but it would get her killed. She wasn't thinking about the fact that seeing Rosa's death was a clear sign; that death was awaiting her. She was ready to gamble with the innocent role rather than give Ayesha peace to her anguish and distraught mind.

"Ayesha, if I'd known who killed your father …" Ariel said then looked Ayesha in her cold eyes. "I would've been had them bitches dealt with. I only agreed to cooperate with the police to avoid being prosecuted in my situation. I would have never testified to show your pops my loyalty. I have a daughter and the only father she has was your father. We all lost a good man, and we're all in pain …"

Could she be right? Ayesha thought almost falling weak until she looked up and saw the evil smirk on Ariel's face who herself didn't realize that her lie was written all over her face.

"You're such a grimy bitch …" Ayesha said as she aimed at Ariel's stomach and pulled the trigger twice.

Psst! Psst!

"Nooo!" Ariel shrilled as she clutched her stomach gasping.

"Who killed my daddy bitch the next lie you give me I will take you to your maker bitch!" Ayesha said to Ariel who was losing a ton of blood. Ariel's hands were imbrued with her blood. She's on borrowed time, this bitch is about to bleed to death. Ayesha concluded as she watched Ariel suffer.

"Tell me Ariel, I will save you. If you had nothing to do with it at least do it for the sake of my daddy having peace —"

"Ayesha ... I told you I can't ..." Ariel said breathless, shaking her head trying to extenuate the burning pain to her stomach.

"So, we gonna play these games to the grave huh?"

"I can't —"

Psst! Psst!

Before Ariel could finish her statement, Ayesha shot her in her chest and shoulder. To her surprise, Ariel was still hanging in there.

She's a fighter, Ayesha thought then saw the blood trickling from Ariel's mouth. Ariel eyes were opened as she was gasping trying to speak. Her lips were moving with no sound emanating.

"Say it Ariel ... tell me damnit?" Ayesha became distraught.

"Youngin' ..." Ariel said clearly causing Ayesha's head to spin, Ariel's chest heaved once then she took her last breath.

"What did you just say?" Ayesha asked a dead Ariel as her knees gave out on her. Ayesha was hit with an overwhelming flash back of ten years ago when she sat on her father's lap.

"Youngin' ... my connect name is Juan, the same Juan from Benz Carlot —"

Boom! Boom! Boom!

Ayesha flinched as if she was seeing it go down again.

"Let's go Fat Boy," the voice of Youngin' played in her head retrospectively.

She now knew why the eyes of her lover looked so familiar.

"Youngin'," Ayesha exclaimed then found her legs, and vanished off into the young night.

To Be Continued ...

CPSIA information can be obtained
at www.ICGtesting.com
Printed in the USA
LVOW13s0917040318
568590LV00011B/661/P